THE ANGEL AND THE AGENT

A SPIES LIKE US BOOK, 2

VANESSA GRAY BARTAL

DRY CREEK PRESS

PROLOGUE

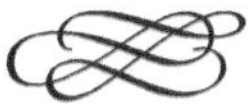

"I have an announcement." Maggie Eldridge stood on a chair to get her friends' attention. "Out of a thousand applicants, my beautiful, sweet, talented, and amazing little sister, Amelia Anne Eldridge, was selected to apprentice at DC's most exclusive salon. She'll be moving here in a month, and I wanted you all to meet her so she'll feel like she knows people." She pointed to Amelia who gave a little wave. She had met many of Maggie's friends before, some of them a few times, but she still felt self-conscious to be the center of attention.

"Also, Cam and I are engaged," Maggie added quickly, revealing the hand she'd been hiding all afternoon.

There were cheers and applause. Someone pulled Maggie off the chair for a hug. Amelia slipped through the excited crowd of well-wishers to the blue-haired man standing alone at the edge of the group.

"How's it going, Papa Smurf?" she asked, linking her arm with his.

"Super," Blue replied. Amelia couldn't tell if his tone was sarcastic or sad. She had no idea how her sister could be so perceptive about everything but the men in her life. Amelia had sensed Blue's feelings for Maggie the first moment she met him. And now she was engaged to another man, their boss no less. It had to be painful, despite the fact it had been coming for the last six months of Maggie and Ridge's relationship.

"Take a walk with me, some distance will help," Amelia said, tugging his arm.

"You're the most adorable little thing," Blue said, resting his arm companionably on her shoulders. "If you weren't so fresh out of pubescence, I'd fall for you too, keep all my unrequited heartbreak in the same family."

"It would be an honor to crush your heart. And your spirit," Amelia said, and he laughed.

"Be honest, has a girl like you ever experienced unrequited love?" Blue asked.

"Honestly?" she said. "No. But one time my brother, Darren, slammed my hand in the car door, and I'm guessing it feels kind of the same."

"I don't know, I've never slammed my hand in a door," Blue said.

"My car's right there. Hold out your hand and then you'll be able to compare," Amelia said.

"What do they put into you Eldridges to grow such wicked senses of humor?" Blue asked.

"Our mother is southern, so basically she specializes in baking and backhanded insults," Amelia said. They chatted as they walked a half-mile down the road, with Amelia doing her best to amuse and distract him, and then the strap on her ridiculously strappy sandals snapped, rendering her shoes useless.

"Are those shoes made of papier-mâché and gossamer?" Blue asked, stooping to inspect them.

"Also gold, if the price is any indication, but look how pretty," she said, staring in disappointment at her ruined shoe.

"Come on, baby possum, I'll give you a ride back to the den," Blue said, bending to allow her to hop on his back.

"You're going kind of slow," Amelia said, poking him after a moment of walking.

"You look slim, but the fact that my ankles and vertebrae are slowly collapsing like an accordion tells me you weigh more than I initially thought," he said.

"This is the worst pony ride ever," Amelia complained.

"You're like one of those kids who pokes the pony with a stick and then sues the owner after it kicks you in the face," Blue said.

"And that is the story of my tenth birthday," Amelia said, forcing him to lean against a tree and laugh. They were almost back at the party now. Amelia tapped Blue's shoulder.

"Give me a second, I'm trying to suck enough oxygen into my lungs to make it the last few steps," Blue said.

"No, who is that?" she asked, spying a latecomer to the party.

Blue looked up and squinted.

"That's Ethan."

"Who is Ethan?" Amelia said. "Besides the future father of my children, I mean."

"No, no, no, baby bear. Ethan is one of Ridge's SEAL buddies, and he is totally off limits to you."

"But he's so pretty," Amelia whispered. He had dark hair and a lopsided, boyish smile that, even from so far away, radiated naughtiness and amusement.

"Yes, and he knows it. Ethan's not the kind you take home and try to litter train. He's the kind you visit in the zoo because he's too wild and dangerous to be a pet. Listen to your big brother Blue and stay away from that one."

Blue deposited her by the drink table. Despite his warning, Amelia couldn't seem to take her eyes off the mysterious Ethan. Eventually he turned in her direction and they made eye contact. She smiled, and he smiled in return, a slow curving of the lips that told her the intense attraction she felt for him wasn't necessarily one sided.

Amelia was the first to look away because she was always the first to look away. She knew how to play the game and always came out on top. What she said to Blue was true—she had never wanted a man she didn't eventually get. Men liked her, providing her the luxury of being choosy. But she had never had such an instant, over-the-top reaction to anyone before.

Her eyes landed on the ice bowl she now realized was empty. She grabbed it and carried it inside for a refill. She was at the freezer adding ice when she heard the door open and close behind her.

"You're new," a male voice said, and she didn't have to look to know it was Ethan. Even his voice gave her a little shiver that started at her spine and worked its way out.

"Depends on your definition. I think I'm kind of old," she said, turning to face him.

"Let me guess, you're the caterer," he said, tapping the ice bowl that was now all that rested between them.

"Yes, but only ice. It's a highly specialized industry. Lots of bankruptcies, especially in the winter," Amelia said.

"Uh-oh," Ethan said.

"What uh-oh?" Amelia asked.

"I recognize that sense of humor. You must be Maggie's little sister," he said. "I've heard about you."

"Why is that an uh-oh? Don't you like Maggie?"

"I adore her, but as her boyfriend's friend, that makes any member of her family totally off limits to me," he said.

"Too bad because my brother is single and looking," she said, earning another smile from him. He leaned uncomfortably close to her and sniffed.

"You smell amazing," he said.

"You smell like sweat. Am I making you nervous?"

"Sorry, I was playing football," he said, reaching for a piece of ice from the bowl as he stood upright away from her. "Would you like me to go away, leave you alone?"

"I didn't say I didn't like it," she said, trying hard not to stare at his mouth as he sucked on the ice cube.

"Are you ever going to tell me your name?" he asked.

"You're a stranger. I'm not supposed to talk to strangers," she said.

"I'm Ethan," he said. "Not so strange anymore."

"How do I know you're an invited guest? Maybe you walked in off the street. Maybe you're not safe."

"I'm definitely not safe," he agreed. "But safety's overrated, don't you think?"

Before she could answer, the door opened and Maggie stepped inside. "Amelia? There you are. We're out of ice." She took two steps in and stopped short, her gaze bouncing questioningly between Amelia and Ethan.

"Hey, sweets," Ethan said, tossing her a wink.

"You're subdued," Maggie said, her tone loaded with suspicion. "Are you sick?"

"Football. Your boyfriend wore me out," Ethan replied.

"Fiancé," Maggie replied, holding her hand aloft and wiggling her ring finger.

"No way, LT made it official? He never said a word."

"He was going to tell you this afternoon, but I subverted his party for this one," Maggie said. She had thrown the party together last minute after Ridge's proposal the night before, as a way to celebrate and let their friends meet Amelia before she went back home for the final time.

"This one's way better," Ethan said, his gaze landing quickly on Amelia and then away.

"Have you met my sister?" Maggie asked.

"Your sister? I was under the impression she was here for the ice. I guess that explains the family resemblance," Ethan said, his wicked smile lighting on Amelia as he spoke.

Maggie's smile dimmed. "She's my baby sister, Ethan. *Baby.* She's way too young, and you're way too old."

He held his hands up in surrender. "You know me, Maggie. I was being friendly."

"People are waiting for the ice." Maggie took the bowl from Amelia and gave Ethan what could only be described as a warning look. He held up his hands again and aimed for an innocent expression. Shaking her head, Maggie headed back outside.

Ethan took a step back and reached for a bottle of water. "How young is young, Miss Amelia?"

"Twenty two."

"Your sister's right; you're a baby, way too young and innocent for an old guy like me," he said. Smiling, he unscrewed the water bottle and took a drink.

"How old is old, Mr. Ethan?" she replied.

"Twenty seven," he said.

She grimaced. "Yikes. How are you hips holding up? I hear those knee replacement surgeries are no joke."

He leaned against the counter, smiling the smile that made her heart do the thing, his legs crossed at the ankles. Thanks to the pickup football game he'd just abandoned, his shirt was slightly wet with sweat and stuck to his chiseled chest. Without her permission, Amelia's gaze traveled from the smile to the chest down to his well-formed calves and back up again. When she reached his face, he was giving her a knowing look. "I do all right."

"I think you should know I'm a good girl," Amelia said.

"I could guess that you were," Ethan said.

"My mom is big on ladylike behavior. I don't kiss strangers, and I never throw myself at men."

"Is there a reason you're telling me this?" Ethan asked.

"I thought you should know what I'm about to do is highly out of character," she said.

His smile widened. "What are you about to do?"

"This," she said and then pushed him into the pantry with her and closed the door behind them.

"I can't believe you're taking the plunge, LT." Ethan stared at his friend in his tuxedo, the reality of his wedding finally sinking in.

"Time to put down roots, son," Ridge said, adjusting his already perfect bowtie in the mirror.

"Why?" Ethan asked. He had known Cameron Ridge for six years, since he was a newbie SEAL. Ridge had been his team leader a mere two years before he optioned out of the navy and transitioned to the world of government espionage. At first he had hated the guy, mostly because he had hated any form of direction or discipline. But after a bumpy start, the two men had become friends, the sort who stayed in contact and remained buddies even after Ridge became a civilian. He had been present for the beginning of Ridge's relationship with Maggie, had even aided in her rescue once, but marriage was a whole other level. How could anyone be ready to settle down when there was so much fun to be had in the world?

"If you have to ask the question, you wouldn't understand the answer," Ridge said. "How's the new job?"

"You're about to get married, and you want to talk about my job?" Ethan asked.

"I need the distraction," Ridge admitted.

Ethan grinned. He was loving seeing his friend so nervous. He had once seen the man as an emotionless rock, the sort who could take out an enemy assailant in the morning and calmly have a cup of coffee in the afternoon. And now he was quaking in his boots because of a wedding. "The job's good, I guess. Not as many thrills as I might have hoped." He missed the SEALs, if he were being honest. Back then his objectives had been clear, as had his motives. He had been fighting for freedom, for protection. The new world, the world of government espionage, was more shades of gray. Sometimes he wasn't certain he was one of the good guys, and he hated that.

"There's a learning curve for each new venture," Ridge told him.

"Are you talking to me or yourself?" Ethan asked.

"Maybe both. I've never been a husband before," Ridge admitted.

"And someday after that you'll be a daddy," Ethan added helpfully.

Ridge grimaced. "Are you trying to make me puke? I've haven't been this jumpy since my SEAL test."

Ethan guffawed. "You know there's a simple solution here: don't get married."

"That's not an option," Ridge said.

"Maggie got you over a barrel with ultimatums?" Ethan guessed.

Ridge gave him a quelling glare. "You think I'm nervous because Maggie's making me do this? Nah, son, you got it all wrong. I wanted to marry her almost from the minute I met her. I just don't want to mess it up. I don't want to let her down."

Ethan had no reply to that. He had known a lot of women and never been tempted to make it permanent with any of them. As for letting someone down, that was how Ethan lived his life. He was a screwup, at least when it came to relationships. A trail of broken, wounded hearts littered his past and, truth be told, he didn't much care. That was how it was, how it was supposed to be. He was the catch that couldn't be pinned down, but he was up front about it, never fooling a woman into thinking they had a chance at something permanent with him. Not his fault if they got too attached.

"You were made for marriage," Ethan reassured him in a rare, serious moment. "You're that steady sort, LT. Husband material, Grade-A."

Ridge blew out a breath and turned away from the mirror. "Tell anyone I was this nervous, and I'll snap your neck."

Ethan grinned. This was more like the man he knew. "Good thing I got it all recorded on my phone."

"I know people who can make you disappear," Ridge warned.

"I know the same people, and I'm pretty sure they like me better," Ethan rebutted. The door opened and they were joined by Ridge's older brother. Calhoun Ridge was the sort of man who entered a space and made everyone else shut up. Even Ethan was intimidated by him, and he wasn't intimidated by much. But the man owned approximately half of south Texas and was likely a millionaire, after having played pro ball and marrying a beauty contestant.

"How's the little guy holding up?" Cal asked, squeezing the back of Ridge's neck. Ridge was nearly six two, but his older brother had a good two inches on him, making him seem small in comparison. The two brothers were six years apart, a mercy that kept them from being as competitive as they might have been. Ridge was a nice looking guy, a practically perfect physical specimen, former SEAL, and high-ranking government operative. And yet he paled in comparison to his seemingly perfect older brother.

"Good, I'm good," Ridge insisted, shooting Ethan a challenging glance in case he might get any ideas about sharing the details of their conversation.

"We were talking about learning curves and changes," Ethan offered. Before Ridge could reach for him and make good on snapping his neck, he hastened to add, "I started a new job recently. LT was talking me through it."

"Ah, good stuff," Calhoun said, not really listening. His affection for his little brother was genuine, but he didn't seem to care about any of the other people in Ridge's life, with the possible exception of Maggie. For a moment Ethan worried about Maggie, wondering what her life would be like as the younger sister-in-law of Calhoun Ridge and his beautiful wife, Isabel. But the concern only lasted an instant. Maggie had a way of warming even the coldest heart; she'd be fine.

The wedding coordinator opened the door and shoved her head inside. "Ready, boys?"

No one had called him a boy since he was a boy, but Ethan didn't mind when the plump and pleasant little old lady did it. She was some distant cousin or friend of Maggie. It seemed like everyone in Maggie's world was friendly and charming and he liked them immensely, at least the ones he had met. Everyone on Maggie's side of the aisle seemed warm and cuddly compared to the SEALs, agents, and Calhoun and Isabel on Ridge's side.

The music began. Ridge and Calhoun took their place at the front of the church, leaving Ethan and Maggie's brothers, Darren and Johnny, to walk their bridesmaids down the aisle. Darren was as quiet and bookish as Johnny was friendly and outgoing. Ethan had never known anyone with Down Syndrome before, and if they were all like Johnny, then he hoped to know several more people in the future. Now, as he stood in the back of the church waiting for his turn to walk his bridesmaid down the aisle, he was so excited over the prospect of being a groomsman that the wedding coordinator had to hush him twice.

"Ethan, can you believe we're part of the wedding?" Johnny asked, grasping his bicep as he shook Ethan's hand for the fourth time that day.

"It's like living in a dream, Johnny," Ethan said, patting Johnny's shoulder. "You'd better get back in line; your turn is coming in a few minutes." Dutifully, Johnny found his place in line and pressed his lips together, bouncing excitedly on the balls of his feet. Smiling, Ethan faced forward and held out his arm to his bridesmaid, a college friend of Maggie's whose name he kept forgetting. The wedding coordinator opened the door and shooed them through, and then it was Darren's turn with his bridesmaid, and finally Johnny and his bridesmaid.

When the maid of honor walked down the aisle, Ethan tried hard to catch her eye, but she seemed to look everywhere but at him. The omission was purposeful, Ethan knew, and he had it coming. When he first met Amelia, Maggie's little sister, he had been immediately and sizzlingly attracted to her. She had all the same warmth he enjoyed about Maggie with a higher dose of stylish sophistication. Where Maggie was all doe-eyed soft and sweet cuteness, Amelia was outright hot. The first time Ethan met her he'd been smitten, so much that, after a few minutes of flirting, the two of them wound up having a steamy makeout session in Maggie's pantry. She gave him her number. He promised to call, but of course he hadn't. They hadn't seen each other until yesterday, six months later. Last night Ethan avoided her, and she made it easy for him to do so. Now, seeing her in her strapless bridesmaid dress, he wondered what the chances were that they could find another pantry.

He zoned out during the wedding. Yes, it was nice and sweet and blah, blah, blah, but it was so far outside of his comfort zone that he couldn't tune in, couldn't grasp what they were saying. Promising to love only one person forever—what was that about?

When the wedding was over, it was time for pictures, a task made less tedious by the fact that separate pictures had already been taken. Now they only had to take the together pictures, and then it was off to the reception hall. Ethan tried to place himself next to Amelia in the limo, but she kept herself busy arranging Maggie's dress and hair. She tried to make it seem as if she weren't purposely ignoring him, but he could tell that she was, and it gave him hope. If she had no attraction to him at all, she wouldn't have worked so hard to ignore him. She was younger than he was, only twenty two, and she was his friend's new little sister, thanks to today's vows, but that only made her more tantalizing to Ethan. He always wanted what was off limits, what he couldn't have.

When at last the requisite groomsman duties were over and the meal had been eaten, it was time to dance. Ethan decided to play it cool. If he rushed over to Amelia and asked her to dance, she would have the advantage. He would hang back, give it a while and then maybe he would get around to asking her for a dance. But as he hung back, admiring his brilliance and cool reserve, another man darted to the forefront and asked her to dance. The man looked familiar, and at last Ethan recognized him as Piedmont Bonvoy, a DC area lawyer famous for getting giant corporations out of sticky situations. He was young, wealthy, locally famous, and considered one of DC's most eligible bachelors. Ethan watched with distaste as he and Amelia danced together, talking and laughing like old friends. And then, as they danced a second and then third song together, Piedmont's hands smoothed up and down Amelia's waist and Ethan had the dawning realization this wasn't their first meeting, that perhaps Piedmont was Amelia's date, that perhaps they were actually *together*.

He glared at them, gobsmacked. How dare she move on from their flirtation when he was just getting into it? And with Piedmont Bonvoy, no less. Ethan was a confident man, perhaps even cocky, but even he found Piedmont Bonvoy slightly intimidating. The man was a genius, a literal genius who graduated law school at the age of nineteen. And, unlike many young geniuses, he had the charm to back up the brains. There was nothing socially awkward or backwards about Bonvoy. And, okay, maybe his muscles came from a gym and trainer, but the guy was ripped.

Ethan stared at the duo, shamelessly pouting. During a turn, Amelia's eyes landed briefly on him and then away. When she almost immediately paused her dance and walked away from Bonvoy, Ethan sat up and took notice. Had that been a signal to him? Did she want him to follow her? Was that what her look had been about? Never one to waste an opportunity for adventure, Ethan darted to his feet and followed, interrupting her brother Darren who was in the middle of a boring story about a comic book convention.

He tailed her as she exited the reception, went into the kitchen and darted into a small room. The sign over the door read "Pantry." *Yes.* Ethan smiled as he stepped inside the room and closed the door behind them.

CHAPTER 2

Amelia was parched. The day had been long and exhausting. She had been so focused on Maggie there had been little time for self-care. But that was how it should be, and she knew one day Maggie would do the same for her, if it ever became her turn. She thought of Piedmont Bonvoy and had to calm the nervous flutters in her stomach. They weren't there yet; they might never be there. They had only been dating a few weeks. Amelia hadn't even been certain she should invite him as her date for the wedding, but when she'd brought it up, Piedmont had seemed enthusiastic.

But after three dances with him, she suddenly realized how incredibly thirsty she was. When was the last time she'd had a glass of water? Her throat felt dry, her skin felt dry, and her lips felt especially dry. If she planned to do any kissing later, and she definitely did, then she needed hydration, stat.

"Well, well, well. Amelia Eldridge, we meet again."

Amelia knew who spoke the words before she turned to look. She stood upright, the bottle of water grasped tightly in her fingers. *Ethan.* Six months ago she'd had a major crush on him. And then, after a blush-inducing makeout session, he had disappeared off the radar.

She had dreamed about him seemingly forever after that, but those days were over now. He'd had his chance, and he'd blown it.

She whirled to face him with a light smile, revealing none of the irritation she felt in his presence. "Ethan, nice to see you. Maggie and Ridge got their perfect wedding, don't you think?" She took a step forward, intending to bypass him, but he put out a hand, halting her progress.

"Where are you rushing off to?" he asked.

"I got my water, and I'm heading out," she said, holding the bottle aloft for his inspection. They'd been out of water bottles in the reception hall, but a helpful waitress had indicated there were more in the pantry. "Did you want one?"

"Water, right," Ethan said, his gaze falling to her lips. "Isn't this the pantry? That's kind of our thing, you know?"

What was he talking about? Did he genuinely believe she'd lured him to the pantry for a repeat makeout session, that all pantries were now connected to him in her mind?

"Are you for real?" she blurted.

"You can't tell me you haven't thought about that night in Maggie's pantry," Ethan said. "I know I have."

Amelia was speechless, and it took a lot to leave her speechless. Did he really believe she'd been pining for half a year, six months in which they'd had no contact after he promised to call her? Okay, it had been her idea to go into the pantry in the first place, but he'd been a willing participant. And if she hadn't started something, he would have. Their attraction had been mutual, as had their flirting. The only difference was that Amelia believed it was heading somewhere when it clearly wasn't.

"I must have missed your call," Amelia said. People like Ethan got away with bad behavior because they were handsome and charming, but Amelia was having none of it.

"Life's been busy," he said. "I started a new job."

"So did I. And I finished school, and I moved cross-country to a new city, got a new apartment. And yet I called everyone I was supposed to," she said.

"Hmm," he said, his eyes still on her lips. It was obvious to Amelia he wasn't hearing a word she said, so she decided to speak his language. She grasped his shirt, drawing him closer so they were toe-to-toe, chest-to-chest.

"I was thinking," she said.

"Yeah?" His eyes glazed as his hands slid to her waist. Clearly he thought this was leading somewhere fun.

"I'd like to see you again."

"You would?"

She nodded. "But this is my sister's wedding. I don't want to risk any sort of distraction on her day."

"What did you have in mind?" he asked.

"Maybe sometime you could show up at the salon when I'm about to end a shift." Her hands slid to his shoulders. "I could slip a cape on you." He nodded again, more enthusiastic this time. Her hands threaded into his hair and she stood on her toes until her lips were almost but not quite brushing his, and she whispered. "And then I could color the gray out of your hair."

He blinked a few times. "Wait, what?"

"Your hair." She rifled his scalp with her fingers. "You should let me color it."

"What? Why would I do that?"

"Because of the gray," she said.

"I'm not going gray," he argued.

She plucked a gray hair and handed it to him, taking a step out of his embrace as she did so. "It's looking a little more salt than pepper up there, but maybe that's the way you like it. With your coloring, you could totally pull off gray hair. Of course you might have to change your handle, but 'Silver Fox,' has a certain ring to it." She winked at him and patted his chest. "See you later, Foxy."

When she walked away and left him standing there, dumbfounded and speechless, she had to fight hard not to laugh. Now *that* had been fun, almost but not quite as fun as making out with him in the first place.

Piedmont was waiting patiently where she'd left him. He smiled at her approach. "Everything all right? You were gone for a while."

"Everything is perfect," she said, unscrewing the water to take a few drinks. She wanted to guzzle the entire thing, but her mother's voice rang in her head, reminding her to be a lady. She offered the bottle to Piedmont, but he shook his head, his lip curling slightly. He didn't like to share food or drinks. For Amelia, who had grown up in a family of sharers, that was almost but not quite a strike against him.

"Would you like to dance some more, or are you ready for a break?" he asked.

"Dancing, if you please. I so rarely get the chance anymore," Amelia said.

"I'm going to have to take you to some more charity events. You'll get enough dancing and canapés to last a lifetime."

"What's a canapé?" she asked.

"As far as I can tell, it's a dry piece of toast with some sort of grayish meat on top," he said.

"Mmm, my favorite," she replied, earning a smile from him.

"Did I mention you look especially beautiful tonight?" Piedmont said.

"You may have, but I'll allow another," Amelia replied. She wasn't insecure, but Piedmont was quite the snag. Of all the women in DC, she wondered how she had been the one to catch his eye. It was only by some stroke of luck he'd chosen her salon for his last haircut. She hadn't been his stylist, but she'd been nearby with her own client, chatting happily. New to DC, she'd had no idea who he was until after he asked for her number. Since he was a stranger, she had at first refused. It was his stylist, Julie, who snatched one of Amelia's cards and shoved it into his fingers.

Don't you have any idea who that was, stupid? Julie had hissed after he left. *When Piedmont Bonvoy asks for your number, you give it to him.* They'd been out a handful of times the last few weeks, and each time he seemed more interested than the last. Amelia was fairly certain she liked him, but there was also a part of her that wondered how much she liked him versus how much she liked the idea of him. Either way, she was flattered by his attention.

"I liked your maid of honor speech," Piedmont said, drawing her back to the present. "I should have you write for me next time I have to give one."

"I could only do it if it's for my sister," Amelia said. "She and I go back a ways."

"Your family's nice," he said.

"They seem to like you, too, although it's hard to tell because they pretty much like everyone. I mean, that came out wrong," she tried, frowning.

Piedmont chuckled. "Don't worry about it, I got the gist. They're warm, nice people. And so is their daughter."

"Maggie's sweet," Amelia agreed.

"Maybe everyone else in the room is thinking about Maggie today, but I've only had eyes for the other Eldridge sister," he said.

"Yeah? I'm not familiar with that one. They must keep her in a closet to hide the crazy," Amelia said.

In reply, he kissed her palm before spinning her so quickly she had to grasp his shoulders to keep her balance. When she reoriented herself, she found that she was facing Ethan who stood against the back wall, arms crossed. They locked eyes. He smiled and shook his head, mouthing something. It took a while to work out what he said, and then she got it:

It's on now.

CHAPTER 3

I t was after midnight by the time Amelia was finally able to leave the reception. She tried to get Piedmont to go home without her, but he said he was happy to stay. Knowing how absolutely crazy busy his life was, she didn't take his time or attention for granted. He even pitched in to help clean up after Maggie and Ridge left. Ethan, she noted, was markedly absent for that part.

Piedmont's driver took her home. There was a part of her that couldn't believe she was dating a man who had a driver. *It's a luxury, I know, but it's such a timesaver. I can work while we sit in traffic, and he's the one who has to deal with rush hour stress.*

Amelia had never invited him up to her apartment before, but there was no getting around it tonight. Mostly because he followed her inside her building uninvited. She was nervous about having him see her teeny tiny little studio. DC was an expensive city, and she wouldn't start making good money at the exclusive salon where she worked until after her probation was over. Some of the more senior stylists made six figures. Amelia couldn't wait until it was her turn to do so. Being poor in the city was no fun, especially when her quasi-boyfriend was likely a millionaire.

She paused outside her door. "Piedmont, about my apartment…"

He rested his hands on her shoulders. "Amelia, do you have any idea where I lived during law school?"

"With your parents?" she guessed. He had been a teenager, after all. Some kind of super genius who finished high school at twelve.

"Yes, so you can imagine the sorry state of my dating life. And then when I finally moved out, I had a crummy little walkup over a crack den. Believe me, I didn't start out with a townhouse in Georgetown."

Townhomes in Georgetown were in the millions. "You're not really easing my anxieties here," she told him. She had never seen his home either, and right now she was glad. If she'd actually landed a glimpse of his luxury digs, she'd for certain never be able to let him see her peephole of a dwelling.

He laughed, his thumbs making soothing little circles on her shoulders. "I like you for you, not your apartment."

She stood on her toes and kissed him, wanting to cement the moment before he saw her crummy little abode. One of his hands slid to her neck, pulling her closer, and he kissed her in return. And then her door opened and they nearly tumbled inside.

"Amelia," Ethan said. He sniffled, and she realized he was crying. For a moment, her heart stopped. Had something happened to Maggie and Ridge? "I'm so sorry I disappeared, baby. I freaked out, okay? I just needed a minute to think about things."

"Um…" Amelia said, too shocked for more words.

"Who?" Piedmont said, his head swiveling confusedly between Ethan and Amelia.

"You were right about us; you were right about everything," Ethan continued, swiping his hand under his nose. "I want to give us a try again, and this time I'm going to do it right. I love you, baby, to the moon and back."

Finally, she caught on. She gave his chest a little shove and pointed toward the exit. "Out, get out of my apartment, you bungling burglar."

"What about the baby?" Ethan continued undaunted, pressing his palms to her belly.

She tossed his hands away and gave him another shove. "Go away, Ethan."

"Ethan Jr. needs a father," he called, though he took a step away from them.

"I hate you forever," Amelia called.

"That's not what your lips said in that pantry," Ethan returned. He winked at her and blew her a kiss before casually tossing his tuxedo jacket over his shoulder and heading down the stairs.

When he was gone, Piedmont remained. "Friend of yours?" he asked.

She shook her head. "Friend of my brother-in-law. It's a long story, sort of a running joke between us."

"Huh," Piedmont said. "It seemed like you two know each other rather well."

"No," she contradicted. "I barely know him, I swear. This weekend was only the second time in my life I've ever seen him. It's just…it's how SEALs are. I can't explain their mentality. They do things like that. They're big into jokes and retaliation."

"What was he retaliating for?" Piedmont asked.

"I told him he was going prematurely gray and offered to color his hair," Amelia said.

"Ah, that would do it," Piedmont said. "Where were we?"

"I was about to invite you inside," Amelia said, glancing in her apartment. What had Ethan touched? Knowing him, probably everything.

"Hmm, I don't think that's quite where we left off," Piedmont said and, reaching for her, kissed her again.

The next morning when Amelia's phone rang with an unknown number, she almost didn't answer. On a hunch, she did.

"How's the morning sickness, Baby Mama?" Ethan said. His voice sounded gravelly with sleep. Amelia rolled over and looked at her clock.

"Who calls at seven on a Sunday morning?" she asked.

"A guy who wants to make sure you're sleeping alone," he said.

She groaned and rubbed her eyes. It wasn't too long ago she had been in college and a night owl. Truth be told, she still sort of was.

"By your growl, I can tell you're happy to hear from me. This is me calling you, by the way."

"You're six months too late," she said.

"It's never too late, Amelia," he said. "How long have you been seeing Bonvoy?"

"Hmm, let's see, how many multiple ways can I tell you it's none of your business?" she said.

"I don't see you with him," Ethan said.

"Then you must not have been paying attention last night," she said.

"He's too uptight for you," he continued.

"Opposites attract and all that," Amelia countered. "And, you know, he's a grownup."

"He and I are the same age," Ethan said.

"Yes, but he's an emotional grownup," she said.

"What does a twenty-two year old know about being emotionally mature?" he asked.

"More than a twenty seven year old, apparently," she said, and he sucked in a breath.

"You wound me."

"I wanted to last night," she said.

"I think we both wanted a lot of unspoken things last night," Ethan said. "Have breakfast with me this morning." He sounded as surprised by the invitation as she was.

"Can't," she said.

"Why? Don't tell me you and Bonsnore are exclusive already," he said.

"Making fun of his name is an example of the emotional maturity you don't posses," she said.

"So have breakfast with me."

"No."

"Why not?"

"Because you only want what you can't have," she said.

"Who says I can't have you?" he asked.

"I do," she replied.

"We'll see," he said and disconnected before she could fathom a comeback. She thought that was the end of it, but she should have known better. An hour later, as she was stepping out of the shower, a knock sounded on her door. When she stared through the peephole, she saw Ethan on the other side, basket in hand. Her forehead rested on the door as she tried to think of the best way to make him go away.

"I know you're in there. Don't make me break in," Ethan called.

Sighing, she opened the door a crack. "What are you doing here?"

"Breakfast," he said, holding the basket aloft.

"Ethan…"

"You can't reject a man who brought you croissants."

She shifted. "Croissants?"

"One regular, and one with chocolate," he said.

Overcome by temptation, she reached out a hand toward the basket. Ethan grasped it and pulled her closer until they were chest to chest. "Hey. You wake up even cuter than you go to sleep. How is that possible?"

"Don't do this," she said.

"Do what?" he asked.

"Don't pursue me like this. I know how it is with you."

"How is it with me?" he asked.

"It's what I said on the phone. You want what you can't have. I like to flirt, and I'm attracted to you, but I'm not casual, and I don't want a broken heart."

He blinked at her, shocked by her honesty. "Fair enough, but I still like you, and we have fun. Friends?"

"Can you be friends with a woman?"

"I'm friends with your sister," he pointed out.

"Can you be friends with a woman who's not married to a man who could rip your arms off?" she amended.

"There's a first time for everything," he said. He held the basket aloft again. "Come on, I know you can smell these and you want them."

Against her better judgment, she moved aside and let him in.

CHAPTER 4

Ethan had no idea what time it was when he stumbled into his apartment and fell into bed. Four days in Morocco and two in Egypt had messed up his internal clock so badly that he wasn't sure if it was day or night, and he didn't care. All he wanted was sleep. He closed his eyes, and was immediately sucked into blackness.

Eleven hours later, he woke, yawned, and reached for his watch. It was early morning on a Thursday, an hour before his usual wakeup time. He should hit the gym, go for a run, something, but his body protested. After so many time zones in such a short amount of time with so little sleep thrown in, he would take this morning to rest and recoup. He'd have plenty of time for a run tonight, and possibly a workout, too.

Stumbling to the kitchen, he started a pot of coffee and then stripped and stepped into his shower, relishing the feel of hot water on his dirt-crusted skin. He wasn't sure if he had showered since he left DC. His brain was so fuzzy he honestly couldn't remember. His assignment, tailing an Egyptian ambassador, had turned from a cakewalk into a five-alarm fire when the man met with a known and wanted arms dealer. Instead of simple surveillance, Ethan had ended up in the middle of an international gunfight before ghosting back out of the country the way he'd arrived: unseen.

The last thing he wanted to do was go to work and have meetings and write reports about his time overseas. The bureaucrats would grill him, as they always did. Why couldn't they understand things didn't always go as well in real life as they did on paper? The lack of bureaucracy was one thing he missed about the SEALs. Back then he'd done the job and passed the buck to someone higher up to explain it. Now he was expected to speak for himself, and it was more stressful than he'd imagined it would be.

He stepped out of the shower, dried off, sniffed the towel, and tossed it in the laundry. The smell of coffee permeated his apartment, and he inhaled deeply, feeling more awake already. On autopilot now, he opened his drawer, reached for a pair of boxers, and stopped short. There were clothes in his drawer, but they weren't his boxers. Reaching in farther, he withdrew a handful of lacy women's underwear. Confused, he circled the room in slow motion, searching for an explanation. When none emerged, he walked to his closet and pulled it open. Where his clothes normally were instead hung tidy rows of little girls dress up clothes—tutus, fairy wings, and Cinderella dresses. A quick glance at the floor showed his shoes all gone, replaced by tiny sized dress-up heels in varying colors.

He stalked back to his other drawers and yanked them open. One was filled with bags of cotton candy, another with a tidy stack of bridal magazines. He sat on the bed and put his head in his hands. Was he still asleep or, worse, hallucinating?

His phone buzzed with a text and he reached for it, startled by the unexpected sound. It was from Amelia, and a sinking feeling of dread began to grow in his stomach as he read.

I moved some things into your place to make way for Ethan Jr. Hope you don't mind! XO, Baby Mama.

Where are my pants?? He texted in reply.

In answer, she sent a picture of his clothes with a ransom note. *Bring two chocolate cupcakes to McPherson square at six PM or you'll never see your pants again.*

And if I don't? he typed.

In answer, she sent him a gif of a blowtorch.

"She's out of her mind," Ethan said, setting the phone aside. What was he going to do? He had arrived home ahead of his suitcase and, even if he had it, all of his clothes were dirty. The only clothes in the house, besides the lace panties and dress up clothes, were the grimy items he'd worn home and slept in last night. He would have to put those on, go to the store, and buy new clothes to wear to work today. Downing his coffee so quickly he burned his tongue, he threw on his clothes from the night before—clothes that should rightfully be burned after all they'd endured, and jogged a few blocks down the street to a department store, buying a new outfit and a three pack of boxers in record time.

He arrived at work sweaty, rushed, and out of breath, not his usual casual and in-control demeanor for sure. He took a few breaths and pasted on a smile, but inside he was seething. She had gone too far, way, way, way too far. Breaking into his apartment, stealing all of his clothes and shoes, *all of them*, and then replacing them with little girl's dress up clothes and fairy wings. He snickered a laugh, earning a few looks from the people he was sharing the elevator with. Pressing his lips together, he tried to reel it in, but it was too late. The more he thought about it, the funnier it became until, by the time he reached his floor, he was doubled over and laughing out loud. Not since he first joined the SEALs had someone hazed him so badly, and he loved it.

One thing about Amelia, she was never boring. For a guy who had a low threshold for sameness, she was a breath of fresh air. And she wasn't trying because she liked him, because she wanted to be with him or impress him. She was doing it because it was who she was, because it was part of her makeup to be fun and ornery.

He pulled out his phone, snapped a pic of himself, and sent it to her with the caption, *You owe me a hundred bucks for a new outfit.*

She replied immediately. *A hundred bucks for pants, shirt, tie, and underwear? You do your shopping at Hobo Jim's Discount Clothing Club?*

Who says I'm wearing underwear?

She sent him a gagging emoji. *Your tie's too short, BTW. The wide part should hit at your belt.*

Is there no pleasing you, woman?

Pretty sure you know how good you look, no extra flattery from me needed, she replied and he smiled.

Maybe not needed, but always appreciated, he typed.

You look so good I...oops, my battery's dying. Later.

Ethan tucked his phone back in his pocket with a smile that didn't go away for most of the day.

Later, he met her at the park with the designated cupcakes. It had been a long, boring, stressful day of meetings, but all that faded away when he saw her standing beneath the statue, waiting patiently for him.

"Did you bring them?" she asked as he approached.

He held the bakery box so she could see it. "Where are my clothes?"

"You'll get them when the time is right," she said.

He tucked the box back against his chest. "Then maybe you won't get these."

She held her phone aloft, her thumb in the middle of the screen. "One signal from me, and your clothes get it."

He thought she was joking, but, knowing her as he was beginning to, he wouldn't put it past her to follow through and torch his wardrobe. He handed her the bakery box. She opened it and inhaled. "Thank you."

"Wouldn't it have been easier to buy the cupcakes yourself?"

"Yes, but where's the fun in that?" she asked. "I'll see you." She turned to go, but he caught her wrist and yanked her back.

"Where are you going?"

"I have to go, I have a thing."

"Now?" he asked. "I just got here."

She checked the time on her phone. "I can give you ten minutes."

"Thank you, your majesty," he said. They sat on a bench. She opened the box and held out it out to him.

"Cupcake?"

Shrugging, he took one and she took the other. "So, how was your day?" she asked, clinking her cupcake against his in a toast before peeling off the wrapper to eat it.

"It was a day." Now that he was here, sitting on a bench with her and eating cupcakes while the sun shone and birds chirped, he had trouble remembering what had been so bad about his day. "How was yours?"

"Super. I'm officially off probation now," she said.

"What does that mean?" he asked.

"It means I can start making real money without having to give most of it to the salon. It means I can acquire my own clients without being assigned whoever comes up in the queue. It means more chance for advancement, for establishment, for permanency. The chance for better hours, having more autonomy over my schedule."

"It kind of sounds like all your dreams are coming true," he said.

"Pretty much," she agreed, smiling happily as she licked a dab of frosting off her fingers.

Ethan got caught up for a minute staring at her. She was incredibly beautiful, but it was more than an outward appearance that attracted him. She shimmered with confidence and good cheer. She might only be twenty two, but she knew who she was and where she was going, something that made her exceptionally appealing.

"Aren't you going to eat?" she asked when he remained mutely holding the cupcake. Snapping to attention, he peeled the wrapper and devoured it, and then stared at his messy, frosting covered fingers.

Amelia withdrew a tissue from her purse and, instead of handing it to him, leaned closer and wiped his fingers, cleaning him as if he were a little boy. When she was finished with his fingers, she wiped his lips and, smiling, patted his cheek.

"There you go, you're all set," she said.

"Have dinner with me tonight," Ethan blurted.

She leaned away from him and sat back. "I can't, I have a date with Piedmont."

"How can you date a man named Piedmont? What do you call him for a nickname, Piedy? Monty?"

"Why does he have to have a nickname?" she asked.

"Because when you care about people, you give them a nickname. Look, I'll show you." He pulled out his phone and drew up her number.

"Melly," she read. "That doesn't make sense. My name is AMElia, not AMELLia," she said.

"The person who is being nicknamed does not get to determine her nickname and, sometimes when I think of you, I think of you as Melly. So there you go."

"There's no good way to nickname Ethan, either," she informed him.

"Ethan's not my real name," he said, and she sat up in surprise.

"What?"

"It's my handle because I'm from Vermont. You know, Ethan Allen. Guy who gave it to me was some kind of freak history buff. But it stuck hard, and that's what everyone calls me. Even at my new job."

"What's your real name?" she asked.

"Only true insiders know, only the people in my most inner circle, the people I care about a great deal." He paused. "It's Becket."

"That's only one of my most favorite names in the entire world," Amelia exclaimed.

"Yeah?" Ethan asked, smiling.

She nodded. "I always thought..." she broke off, embarrassed.

"You always thought what?" he prodded.

"I always thought if I had a son, I would name him Becket," she admitted a bit shyly.

"What about Ethan, Jr.?" he asked.

She smiled and checked her phone. "I really have to run. Thanks for this, it was nice."

"It was nice," he agreed. "And where are my clothes?"

"They're already back at your apartment. I had to distract you so my accomplices could return them."

"What accomplices?" he asked.

"Shh," she said, touching her finger to her lips. Then she kissed her finger and touched it to his forehead. "Later, Ethan Becket."

"Later, Amelia Melly. Have fun with Piedy."

"The fun goes with me wherever I am," she told him.

"I believe it," he said, his eyes following her long after she walked out of sight.

CHAPTER 5

Slowly but surely, Amelia was building a clientele. The waiting list for an appointment with her grew steadily longer. She felt as if she were climbing her way up the DC social ladder, one client at a time. At first she had started with a few congressional aids and then, as word spread, a few congressman and lobbyists. Next week she had an appointment with a Senator. She wasn't sure where to go after that. Would the president's wife one day make an appointment? Doubtful, but a girl could dream.

DC was an image-based city, and that worked out well for a stylist who made her living based on helping people with their image. Amelia swore to herself when she finally began to arrive, she would be frank with people, telling them honestly when she thought a desired look wouldn't work for them. It wasn't always easy, but she found people appreciated her input. No one wanted to look bad, and if she could somehow stop that from happening, they were willing to pay for her services.

This morning's client was new to the salon and had been waiting for two months to get in. Amelia didn't have much information on her other than the fact that her husband did something with the military. Like everything in DC, it was classified and therefore an open secret.

For instance, Amelia wasn't supposed to know her brother-in-law and sister were spies, but she did. Likewise Ethan had also recently delved into the world of espionage. Amelia knew what his job was, despite the fact that he pretended he worked for a private indexing firm, but she'd never called him on it.

When her client arrived, five minutes early, she turned heads, mostly because she was massively pregnant, so large she looked ready to pop. No wonder she'd been in such a mad rush to get in. Amelia greeted her warmly, offering a hot beverage or cold-pressed juice from the bar.

"No, thank you," the woman, Jordan, said.

Amelia seated her and pulled up a chair beside her so they were face to face. The salon made a big point about individual attention. Each client got the stylist's undivided devotion for as long as the appointment lasted so there was no feeling of being rushed, only of being valued and pampered. "Would you prefer I call you Mrs. Peterson?" Amelia asked.

"Call me Jordan, please," the woman said.

"Jordan, what did you have in mind today? What would you like to have happen in our session?"

"Ideally I'd like some color, but," she paused and pressed her palm to her swollen belly. "That's going to have to wait a bit, according to my doctor. I guess what I'd most like is to feel pretty, despite the bloat and water retention. I need a refresh, a perk. I've gained sixty pounds this pregnancy, and my self-image is taking a beating."

"Hmm," Amelia said, nodding in sympathy. She wasn't faking her pathos; she genuinely couldn't imagine how difficult it would be to gain so much weight in such a short amount of time. "You carry it well, it's all baby. I would never have guessed how much you've gained unless you told me."

"I'm not sure I believe you, but at least it's for a good cause," Jordan said, wincing and groaning as she shifted.

"Are you feeling all right? Can I get you a pillow or prop your feet to make you more comfortable?"

"I don't think anything is going to help at this point. The contractions are seven minutes apart."

Amelia froze. "You're in labor?"

Jordan nodded. "But I've been waiting so long to get in, and I want to look good in the post-baby pictures, you know?"

"Are you sure you want to do this? I could rearrange my schedule to get you in post-baby. I'll even come in on my day off," Amelia said. She didn't do well with people who were sick or in pain. And bodily fluids? Forget about it. It was the number one reason she hadn't gone into medicine in college.

"I'm totally fine," Jordan said. She gripped the edges of the chair and breathed deeply as another contraction took her.

That was way less than seven minutes apart, Amelia thought. But who was she to argue with a pregnant woman? "Let's get started," Amelia said. Her tone sounded rushed, but she couldn't help it. The thought of someone having a baby in her chair terrified her. She washed Jordan's hair, sweating as she tried to maneuver around the woman's giant bump, wincing every time Jordan groaned and gripped the chair. A few surreptitious glances at the clock showed the contractions approximately three minutes apart, at least by Amelia's calculations.

"Is this your first baby?" Amelia asked as she massaged Jordan's hands with oil.

"Mm, hm," Jordan said, breathing heavily through her nose as another contraction hit.

The hand massage portion of things was supposed to take a luxurious half hour, but Amelia only gave each hand five minutes. And at that her own hands were shaking.

"Do you have a name yet?" she asked as she stood and began to gently comb Jordan's hair.

"Yes, but we're not sharing until after he's born," Jordan said, teeth gritted.

Amelia was mirroring her tension. She felt as if everything inside her was clenched and in pain. This was by far the most stressful client encounter she'd ever had, and it had barely begun.

As the session continued, so did Amelia's nerves and so did Jordan's misery. Eventually she gave up on conversation completely and doubled over, moaning in agony. Amelia glanced around the salon uncertainly, hoping for a rescue, but no one seemed to notice what was happening, no one but her supervisor who motioned her over, an angry expression on her face.

"Amelia, what is happening with your client?" Petra snapped.

"She's in labor. I seriously think she's about to have her baby right here," Amelia said. "Can I call an ambulance for her and force her to go?"

"Are you joking? How would that look if word gets out that we force our clients into an ambulance against their will? Just keep her happy, and keep her quiet."

"But she's in *labor*," Amelia said.

"Look, you're new here, but I'm telling you that if she leaves here by any means but the door and with anything but a smile on her face, your head is going to be on the platter," Petra said and turned her back, effectively ending the conversation.

The little talk did nothing to ease Amelia's anxiety. In fact it inched up exponentially to the point she could barely hold the hair dryer and brush for shaking. And it was nearly impossible to dry the hair of a woman who was doubled over panting.

Suddenly Jordan sat up. "Uh-oh."

"Uh-oh what?" Amelia asked, her voice quaking.

"Pretty sure my water just broke," Jordan said. Amelia didn't want to look, but she couldn't help but see the liquid seeping all over the floor. She glanced at Petra for direction, but Petra made a slicing motion across her throat.

"Um, Jordan, I really think maybe you should go to the hospital now." Amelia reached for her water bottle and sipped it, fighting her gag reflex. She really, really, really didn't do well with bodily fluids. Spots appeared before her eyes, and she fought the urge to black out. She sat, fanning herself. "Please," she added weakly.

Jordan began doing the Lamaze pant. She reached out and gripped Amelia's hand, hard. "I'm going to go, but I want you to know the baby's name, in case things go bad at the hospital. Someone needs to tell the doctor."

"But I won't be there," Amelia said.

Jordan's eyes popped open. "You're not coming with me? But my husband is out of town. I have no one else. I don't want to go alone, please."

"Okay, sure," Amelia said. She had no idea how she'd get out of work, but maybe she was fired after this anyway. The room started to spin. She closed her eyes and put her head between her legs.

"The baby's name," Jordan paused and squeezed her hand, breathing hard, "Is Ethan, Jr."

Amelia froze, opened her eyes, and sat up. "What did you say?"

Jordan was now sitting normally and smiling. She pointed to the window of the salon. Amelia turned to look and saw Ethan standing against his motorcycle. He kissed his fingers and waved at her. "It was all fake?" she asked, turning to stare at Jordan in shock.

"I really am pregnant, but I'm not due for another couple of months. And I really did want the appointment with you."

"But you called two months ago," Amelia said. That was way before she pulled her prank on Ethan by stealing all his clothes.

"Ethan's an elaborate game player. The jokes he and my husband used to play on each other are legendary," Jordan said.

"Who is your husband?" Amelia asked.

"Shimmer," Jordan said.

Amelia had heard the name; he was one of Ridge's friends, another former SEAL team member. "I think I might be sick," Amelia said, but she was half laughing. He had gotten her; he had gotten her good.

Petra came over and hugged her shoulders. "I'm sorry, Amelia, but he made it sound so fun when he called to run it by me. Don't hate me."

"I don't hate you," Amelia said, returning her hug. She was immensely relieved that Ethan had run it by her boss first. As long as she wasn't in trouble at work, she could take whatever he threw at her.

She turned toward the front window again to confront Ethan, but he was already gone.

"I've never known Ethan to prank a girl before. You must be something special," Jordan said. Amelia snapped to attention and resumed working on her hair.

"We're friends," Amelia insisted.

"Are you married?" Jordan asked. Amelia shook her head. "I've never known Ethan to be friends with a woman who wasn't married to one of his friends."

"You know his name's not actually Ethan," Amelia said for lack of a better response as Jordan continued to stare speculatively at her in the mirror.

"I know, but no one knows what it actually is. It's kind of become a joke. Not even my husband knows. Maybe Ridge does, but he's never told anyone."

"No one knows?"

Jordan shook her head. "He doesn't like it, thinks it's girly, so he's always gone by Ethan for as long as any of them have known him."

"Wow," Amelia said. She had no idea his real name was a secret; she was glad she hadn't blurted it. The rest of the session was pleasant, now that Amelia knew she wasn't going to have to deliver a baby and the substance in her chair was harmless water. She liked Jordan, and the two agreed to meet for coffee sometime.

"We might as well become friends if our guys are," Jordan noted.

"Ethan and I aren't together," Amelia reminded her.

Jordan smiled. "I've known Ethan a long time. Trust me when I tell you I think we'll be seeing more of each other."

CHAPTER 6

Ethan should have been suspicious when Ridge called instead of texted like usual.

"What's up?"

"What are you doing?" Ridge asked.

Ethan frowned at his phone. "Heading to work." They weren't the sort of buddies who checked in with each other or had long chats about their hopes and dreams.

"Busy tonight?"

"No."

"Let's go out," Ridge said.

"It's my birthday," Ethan said.

"I know, that's why I'm asking."

Ethan resisted the urge to pull the phone away from his ear and look at it. "Are we the type of friends who celebrate each other's birthdays now? Because I might be busy when you call for the next decade or so," Ethan said. "What's this about?"

Ridge let out a breath. "Amelia dragged it out of me. She and Maggie want to go out to celebrate. When I told them you hate your birthday and like to spend it alone, they looked at each other like we'd just seen a puppy get run over in the street."

"Aw, man, that's a nice thought, but I don't celebrate my birthday," Ethan said. He couldn't say for sure why he hated his birthday; he just did.

"The Eldridges are big into birthdays. Believe me when I tell you it will go easier for you if you don't struggle and let it happen."

"You let them make a big deal out of your birthday?" Ethan asked.

"My first birthday with Maggie, she dragged me to a carnival and force-fed me caramel apples and cotton candy. I threw up for the first time in eight years, and it was still the best birthday I've ever had," Ridge said.

Ethan blew out a breath. "Where and when?"

Ridge gave him the name of the restaurant.

"Will you at least try to rein them in?" Ethan pled. "No sombreros and clapping waiters?"

"I think we both know I have no say in the matter. Just show up and don't be late," Ridge directed.

Ethan made it through his workday with no one realizing it was his birthday. The day was so ordinary he would have forgotten the significance of it, except for the fact he'd promised to meet the Ridges and Amelia at the restaurant, a posh, trendy place with outdoor seating and a line around the block.

He was the last to arrive at the restaurant, though he wasn't late. About fifteen people were waiting in line. Ethan expected to have to join them, but when he gave the hostess his name, she directed him to the outdoor patio where Maggie, Ridge, and Amelia were already seated.

"Happy birthday!" Maggie and Amelia called, turning several heads around them. They stood to give him a hug, and Amelia used the opportunity to put a birthday sash on him while Maggie attached a pointed party hat and stuffed a noisemaker between his lips.

"Thanks for getting them to tone it down," Ethan said, promptly removing everything and setting it aside.

"This is the toned down version," Ridge said. "You don't even want to know what I talked them out of."

"Ethan, it's you're *birthday*," Amelia said, as if he didn't know. At least when she spoke it gave him the chance to look at her. She wore a long floral sundress, and her lustrous blond hair was down and fell in soft waves around her face. He had never seen her look better, in fact had never seen anyone look better. With effort, he peeled his eyes away from her. Maggie and Ridge had no idea anything was going on between them, besides a budding friendship. They didn't know how flirtatious the tone of their friendship was, and they certainly didn't know about the kiss that had brought them together in the first place. He and Amelia were careful, incredibly so, not to clue them in that anything was amiss. If they knew, they wouldn't take it well, and rightly so. He was a heartless cad when it came to women, after all. And Amelia was young, fresh, and innocent.

His eyes strayed to her again, and he reeled them back in, focusing instead on the breadbasket beside him. "How'd you guys get in here? Every time I pass there's a crazy long line."

"The owner's a new client of mine, and she said if I ever wanted to get in to let her know and she'd make it happen. I've never done a backroom deal like that before. I feel sort of like a crooked politician," Amelia admitted.

"You're in the right city then," Ethan said, his eyes leaving the bread to land on her again. *She's done speaking, look away*, his brain warned him. He did so, but not before he caught her soft, amused smile, the one that said she knew exactly what was going on with him.

"Why do you hate your birthday, Ethan?" Maggie asked, snagging a piece of bread from the basket beside him. She craned her neck, looking inside it. "Hey, real butter. This *is* a good restaurant."

"I don't know. It never lived up to the hype, you know? When I was a kid, I would have these big fantasies about how it was going to be, that something unexpected and amazing would happen, but then it would be another day. Eventually I stopped wanting it to be anything different," Ethan said.

Maggie blinked at him and gave him the piece of bread she'd just buttered. "You might need this more than I do."

"That sounded more pathetic than I intended," he said, but he accepted the bread and ate it. "Why do you guys like birthdays so much?"

"Because there were four of us, and it was hard to get individual time. Birthdays were our day, the one time a year it was all about us and no one else. We got to feel special and like the center of the universe," Amelia said.

"I was going to say because we got cake," Maggie added. "Plus Johnny loves birthdays. It doesn't even have to be his birthday, he gets so excited over everyone's birthday you can't help but catch the mood. You end up wanting to have a fun, good birthday for him, so you don't let him down."

"Plus we got cake," Amelia seconded, and the sisters bumped fists. The waitress arrived then. They ordered and spent time talking while they waited for their food to arrive. It was a fun, pleasant night, and Ethan was enjoying himself, but he was distracted by Amelia, by her nearness and scent. He was supposed to be becoming immune to her. The more he saw her, the less he should want to see her. That was how it had always worked with women before. He found flaws and ran away quickly. But he couldn't run away from her. She was his friend's sister, and she had become his friend, too. And so she lingered in his circle, tantalizingly close, yet completely out of reach. It was maddening that when he finally developed lingering interest in a woman, she was completely off limits.

It worked to his advantage that she was an expressive speaker, using her hands and body to make a point. Every time she leaned forward or moved back, she brushed his leg, his arm, his thigh. Once he might have believed she made the contact on purpose as a secret signal of her interest. Now he knew better. She had no idea how many times she bumped and brushed him, how closely her chair was aligned with his.

After supper, Maggie presented him with a cake. "Amelia baked it, and I decorated it," she said. It was leaning, sliding, and a little lumpy, but Ethan was deeply touched by their thoughtfulness.

"She's better at decorating than I am," Amelia confessed.

"If Maggie's better at decorating, your cakes must be," Ridge began, but then caught sight of Maggie's expression.

"What, husband? Amelia's cakes must be what?" she prompted.

"Equally delightful and full of love," he said, kissing her cheek.

"Nice save, LT," Ethan said with full admiration. "Thank you for this. And thank you for not bringing candle…oh, I spoke too soon." Amelia opened her purse, pulled out number two and eight candles, and stuck them on the cake. She also removed matches and held them aloft, paused.

"Before we light, you have to make a wish, and before you make a wish, you have to tell us what you wanted to have happen when you were little that never did," she commanded.

"I don't know, really. Something spectacular and amazing, I guess," he said. He rested his arm on the back of her chair as he spoke, using the opportunity to gaze at her face, her warm brown eyes, her cute, slightly upturned nose, her full, perfect mouth. He was fairly certain he knew what his wish would be.

"Okay, now you may blow out your candles." She lit his candles and sat back while he blew them. Almost immediately when he was finished, the man directly behind him stood up and began to loudly sing.

"One day more, another day another birthday gone, how could this one day last so long," and when he was finished another person stood to add to the song, and then another and then the entire line of people waiting to get inside joined in, singing a song from *Les Miserables*, but with different words. Finally, after his initial shock wore off, Ethan realized that not only was it a flash mob, but it was a flash mob for *him*, and they were singing about his birthday.

He sat frozen and mortified, blushing for what had to be the first time in his adult life. At the same time, he was oddly thrilled. They had done this for him, had planned and carried out an elaborate birthday surprise involving thirty people, some of whom had been sitting and dining as long as they had.

The song finished and everyone applauded—not just the singers, but him. "Wow," he said. "So much wow. I was pantsed during the final football game my senior year in front of a stadium of five hundred people, including my grandma. And I think I was less embarrassed then than I was just now. But at the same time that was amazing, so thank you." Under the table, he squeezed Amelia's knee. As much as Maggie also loved birthdays, he knew Amelia had been responsible for the whole evening. It had her fingerprints all over it. She covered his hand, gave it a squeeze, and let go. He followed suit and removed his hand, pressing it to his own leg to keep it from straying back to her.

"So, seeing as how you guys are our closest friend and our closest family, respectively, we have an announcement, and we wanted you to be the first to know," Maggie began.

"You're pregnant," Ethan blurted.

"Are you insane? We just got married, bite your tongue. No, we're getting a puppy." She clapped her hands together excitedly.

"No way," Amelia replied, clapping her hands in the exact same gesture. "What kind?"

"We're getting him from a rescue, so they can't say for certain, but he looks mostly Dane," Maggie said.

"Although they said he probably has some mastiff in him, so he has the potential to be even bigger than a regular Dane," Ridge added with a sarcastic thumb's up.

"I'm going to take a few days off until he gets settled. Ideally, I'd become a stay-at-home mom now, but financially I don't think we're there yet," Maggie said.

"Maybe that will happen when we have an actual child," Ridge said.

"Just because he's adopted doesn't make him any less our child," Maggie argued.

"But the fact that he's not human does," Ridge said.

"That's right, get it out of your system now before he gets here," Maggie said. "Speaking of which, we're picking him up crazy early in the morning, so we're calling it a night."

"I'm going to stay," Amelia said.

"I'll see her home," Ethan volunteered, knowing she had likely taken the Metro to save on parking.

"Are you ready to go home?" he added after Maggie and Ridge

took their leave.

"I'm never ready to go home," Amelia replied.

"Ah, to be young again," Ethan lamented.

"I'm sorry, Grandpa. Remember what it was like to be twenty seven?"

"It feels like yesterday," Ethan mused. "So where do you want to go, party girl?"

"I'm still learning the city, you tell me," she said.

"With people or private?" he asked.

She eyed him, thinking. "Private."

"I know a place," he said, standing.

"Something told me you would." She hooked her index finger through his and allowed him to lead her out of the restaurant. Once outside, they took a few steps and he stopped short.

"What is your face doing?" he asked.

"Smiling?" she tried.

"That's not how you smile. You look like you just stepped on a Lego. Is there a problem?"

"These shoes are killing my feet," she admitted, leaning on a brick wall for support.

"Why did you wear them?" he asked.

"Are you joking? Look how super cute they are," she pointed to her toes, and he looked down.

"It's hard to see them through all the blood," he said.

"Shh, they'll hear you," Amelia said.

"Why do you have to be one of those girls?" he asked, shaking his head.

"Because something tells me if I were wearing support hose and comfortable orthopedics, we wouldn't be here right now," she said.

"We probably would, but I wouldn't have to carry you," he said.

"You're going to carry me?" she asked.

"It's four blocks to my ride because parking was its usual nightmare. I'd prefer not to have you in tears and dragging one foot behind you when we reach my bike. Bad for my image." He crouched, and she jumped on his back.

"Can you carry me four blocks?" she asked.

"Honey, I had to train carrying a buddy three miles at a sprint in full gear. I think I can handle carrying a pretty little girl four blocks," he said.

"Yes, but can you support me and your ego? Seems doubtful," she said, pinching him.

"You make it through BUD/S training and then get back to me on the status of your ego," he challenged.

"Um, hello, I made it through salon school where I had to learn to deal with women who think I'm somehow going to make them look like the picture of the model they walked in with, so I think I know a little bit about stressful situations," she told him.

He laughed. "You're right, it's totally the same. My apologies." They reached his motorcycle, and she slid off his back. He reached into the pocket behind the seat, withdrew a helmet, and fastened it over her head.

"No complaints about this ruining your hair?" he questioned.

"You must think I'm so shallow," she said. "Quick question, can we swing by the salon so I can fix it on the way home?"

He shook his head and helped her onto the bike.

"Um, I'm no safety expert, but this seems like a catastrophe waiting to happen, unless that's your grand plan to do away with me," she said, flapping the folds of her long, ankle-length dress.

"May I?" he asked, holding the skirt in his hands.

"Sure," she said, her tone wary. She watched as he tied the skirt into a tidy bundle so it wouldn't hang over the wheels.

"Okay?" he asked.

"Yes, as long as it's not one of those complicated sailor knots I'm going to be stuck with forever," she said.

"It's a simple figure eight," he said.

"The fact that you know the name of the knot is sort of hot. Maybe I *am* attracted to nerds," she mused.

"I'm glad I could help you along with your journey toward self-discovery," he said. She laughed. He hopped on the motorcycle, and they took off.

CHAPTER 7

Ethan wound through traffic at a dizzying speed. Amelia held on to his waist, pressing her cheek to his back. Eventually they stopped. She sat up and looked around at a part of the city she'd never seen before. He took her hand to help her off the bike.

"Okay?" he asked.

"Perfect," she replied. "I love motorcycles. My friend from back home had one and used to sneak me for rides whenever my mother wasn't looking. Sadly, she was almost always looking."

"You seemed a little frightened," he said.

"No, I wasn't scared at all," she said.

"That's strange because you were holding on tightly, pressing against me, almost like you were trying to melt into me," he said.

She was glad it was growing dark so he couldn't see her cheeks heat with a blush. "I was under the impression that was proper motorcycle passenger etiquette."

"I guess that explains why your friend used to try to give you so many rides," he said.

"Her name was Shelly. Things got awkward," she said, and he laughed.

He led her up some steps and then they climbed for a bit until at last they spilled out onto a cliff overlooking the Potomac. All around them graffiti had been sprayed on the rock walls. It wasn't the sort of place Amelia would frequent by herself, but with him she felt safe. Scary people might come to this place, but Ethan was far more lethal than anyone they might encounter. They sat and watched in silence as the sun sank low over the river.

"Beautiful," Amelia murmured.

"It is," Ethan agreed.

"Come here often?" she asked.

"Nah. When I was a kid and used to travel to DC for various reasons, I scouted out all the cool, out-of-the-way hangouts. Now that I'm elderly and settled, I don't have time to revisit them. I probably haven't been here in five years."

"Since you were my age," she reminded him. "What were you like then? How have you changed? Because sometimes it's hard to imagine being any different than I am now, but I know people grow and mature as they get older."

"Not all people do. Some people seem stuck in a perpetual childhood, like Peter Pan. Only the really good ones are constantly growing and changing," he said.

"True," she agreed. "So, tell me, how have you grown and changed?"

"I used to have a bigger chip on my shoulder, like I had something to prove to the world. I don't feel that way anymore. I've learned to let a lot of little things go, to not view every cross word or piece of advice or discipline as a threat to my manhood."

"So you were a hothead," she clarified.

"Yes, and thank you for using the past tense on that. I've been trying to do better on that front."

"You've succeeded. I don't view you that way at all."

"How do you view me?" he asked, grinning.

She regarded him but didn't answer. He poked her leg, albeit gently. "Still waiting."

"Settle in, it's going to be a long wait," she said.

"Is there a particular reason you don't want to answer the question?" he asked with a cocky, knowing smile.

"Would you answer, if I'd asked you how you view me?" she challenged.

"Yes," he said.

"Go ahead then," she said, leaning back onto her hands as she awaited his answer.

"You, Amelia Eldridge, are like one of our famous cherry blossoms in the spring. Bright, colorful, beautiful, attractive, good smelling, sweet. And the temptation is there to think that's all there is, a pretty little flower. But then winter comes and the blossoms fade, and you see the true beauty of the tree, the way the branches spread and the trunk twists, and you realize the tree must have crazy deep roots to produce that kind of fruit, year after year after year."

"Okay, I was expecting something flippant, and you almost made me cry. Thank you," she said.

"It's still your turn," he prompted.

"I can't," she said.

"Why not?"

"Because I'm seeing someone, and it wouldn't be fair to him."

"Now I'm a little glad you won't say because what I'm imagining is probably better than the reality," he said.

"Believe me, it's not," she said. The atmosphere bottomed out between them and the usual tension that was at a simmer suddenly jumped to a rolling boil. They remained silent for a moment, waiting for things to return to normal.

"What do you and Piedmont do on dates?" he asked after a while.

"He has a lot of social engagements, work events, charity things, networking stuff. It's a lot of dressing up, going to parties, dancing, eating tiny food."

"That sounds right down your alley," he said. "Getting fancy, dancing, eating."

"At first it was fun. No, it was a blast. But I'm kind of reaching that point where I've rotated the same three dresses so many times I'm either going to have to spend a paycheck on a new dress or get a reputation as some kind of frugal clothes recycler. And the food isn't as good as you might imagine. They make it ahead of time in mass quantities, so by the time I eat it, it's lost all flavor and appeal. The dancing's always fun, but Piedmont has to spend so much time talking to so many people we're lucky to eke out one dance per event." She paused. "Listen to me, complaining because the gourmet food is bland and my clothes aren't posh enough. First world problems much, Amelia? Sorry, I wasn't trying to complain. It *is* fun. I guess I was making the point that not everything is as shiny as it appears, even fancy parties."

"But you and Piedmont get along?" he prodded.

"Absolutely. He's by far the best, most attentive guy I've ever gone out with, but not in a cloying way, you know? It's like the perfect amount of attention and space. He's kind, funny, thoughtful, smart, interesting. I find myself cynically searching for flaws because, so far, he seems like the perfect man. I feel lucky he's turned his attention to me when he could have anyone in this city."

"Wow, that was fun, thanks for the information. Be right back, going to go cut off my ears now," he said.

She laughed. "You asked."

"That's because I'm a moron. Plus I was hoping you'd highlight all his flaws, tell me he's boring and picks his teeth with matchbooks, yells at waiters, makes small children cry. Instead he sounds like a less-pudgy Buddha."

She laughed again, clutching her stomach. "Oh, Ethan. You're so funny."

"Super. Your boyfriend's a saint, and I rank up there with Zippo the Clown."

She laughed harder. "Stop it. You're going to make me tinkle."

"Amelia, I've been on submarines with sailors whose language could peel the skin off an armadillo, so when you say 'tinkle' in normal conversation, it's the oddest and most adorable thing ever."

"You can thank my mom for that. She was very choosy about how we were allowed to talk at home. She called bad language 'talking blue.' I still have no idea what that means, but anytime we encountered someone cursing in public, she would literally take our hands and steer us around them announcing, 'Let's walk this way, girls, they're talking blue.'"

"I love that. I can picture little you and little Maggie all wide-eyed at some foulmouthed street person," he said.

"Yes, but what you don't realize is how extensive her barred vocabulary ran. In addition to curse words, we weren't allowed to say anything she considered crude. To this day, I have never once uttered the word f-a-r-t."

"Are you joking?"

"I just spelled it, and you think I'm joking."

He closed his eyes, smiling. "You're like the antidote to military life."

"Wait, you mean to tell me that people in the military actually say the word f-a-r-t?" she asked.

"And sometimes darn," he added, and she gasped.

"Somewhere my mother is crying, and she doesn't know why. You should have seen her when Johnny went through the phase where he didn't know curse words were bad. Kids at school would tell him things to say, so he'd come home and blurt them at dinner. My dad almost had to Heimlich my mom four times that year."

"Little punks," Ethan groused. Having met Johnny, he'd do serious damage to anyone who tried to hurt or take advantage of him.

"Maggie took care of them," Amelia said.

Ethan laughed. "Maggie? Sweet, sugar-loving Maggie?"

"Clearly, you've never seen her angry."

"What did she do?"

"She was an office aid, so she slipped a paper into the announcements and had them called to the science lab. When they got there, she'd taped a note stating that the principal wanted to meet with them and it was serious so they'd better sit down and shut up. Then she taped a note on the outside of the door saying someone had thrown up and everyone should stay away until the janitor could get to it. It was Friday, and our janitor had Fridays off because he came in Saturdays and did a big clean. Anyway, our science lab could be padlocked from the outside because it had so much expensive equipment and chemicals in it. So she locked them in. Everyone went home. This was before cellphones were ubiquitous in school, so they had no way to make contact. They weren't found until almost midnight, after their parents raised the alarm and someone finally figured it out and tracked them down."

"Geez," Ethan said, laughing. "Did she get in trouble?"

"She got suspended, but only for one day because the principal liked her and the kids were jerks. And they never bothered Johnny again."

"I have new respect for your sister," he said.

"She looks sweet and cuddly, but don't underestimate her."

Ethan nodded, agreeing for reasons she couldn't know. The first time he'd gone shooting with Maggie and Ridge remained one of life's more shocking events. The woman could probably shoot an ant off a dime, given the opportunity. *Feeling bad about yourself as a trained operative, huh?* Ridge had asked when the afternoon was over. *And as a man,* Ethan had added.

They talked for a long time, until it grew so chilly she began chafing her hands up and down her arms for warmth, until Ethan began surreptitiously checking his watch and calculating how few hours sleep he'd get before work.

"We can go," Amelia said, the third time she saw him sneak a glance at his wrist.

"I'm sorry. If I didn't have work tomorrow..." he let the thought trail off and grimaced. "I really am an old man now."

"Don't worry about it," Amelia said, stifling a yawn. "Maybe I'm getting old, too."

He held out his hand to her, and she took it, allowing him to help her up. They had been talking so long her legs were numb and night had fully fallen. The moon was a speck, barely providing enough light to line their path. Amelia turned to Ethan to say something, but the words stuck. His face was rigid, tense, expectant.

"What..." she began but he let go her hand and turned, facing a man who had come up fast behind them. Amelia hadn't even heard him approach until it was too late. Ethan, however, was prepared. The man's hand barely had time to emerge from his coat pocket before Ethan grabbed it, twisted it behind the man's back, and shoved him face first against one of the graffiti-strewn cliff walls. He frisked the man, spreading his feet apart with one leg.

"What are you doing, man, I was just out for a walk. I wasn't doing nothing," the man said, breathing hard as Ethan squeezed the air out of his lungs. His words confused Amelia. As far as she could tell, the man had done nothing wrong except walk too close to them. Did Ethan have some kind of hair trigger that could be set off by someone invading his personal space?

Then he pulled a gun out of the man's waistband, along with several wallets from his pockets and a wicked looking knife. He palmed the gun, chuckling. "What is this piece of garbage? Did you steal your grandma's gun to rob people?"

The man's tone changed. He began hurling a few nasty epithets at them until Ethan wrenched his arm tighter, ending the tirade by making the man squeal in pain.

"Are you going to run away like the scared piece of human waste you are, or do I have to break your arm?" Ethan asked, giving the arm another twist.

"I'll go, I'll go," the man cried. Ethan released him. Sniveling, he took a step back and rubbed his arm. "Can I have my stuff back?"

"I'm going to give all these wallets to the police so they can go back to their rightful owners. Do you want your gun back?" Ethan asked.

The man nodded.

"Absolutely," Ethan replied before hurling the gun over the cliff and into the Potomac. "Go and get it. You want some help?" He took a step toward the man who ran off whimpering, disappearing into the inky blackness.

"Um..." Amelia said. It was the first thing she'd uttered since the ordeal began. Ethan seemed to come back to himself and remember she was there.

"So...sorry about that." He scratched behind his ear, seeming to have no idea what to say next.

"Um, that was..." Amelia began again, but she also seemed unable to continue.

"Disturbing?" he guessed. "I'm sorry you had to see that."

"Yes, disturbing. That's the word I was searching for. I find you deeply, incredibly disturbing right now. Icky. Yuck."

He laughed and held out his hand to her so they could resume the walk to his bike. "I didn't even hear that guy. How did you know he was coming, and how did you know he was going to try and rob us?"

"Years of training. You get a sense about people and their intentions," he said. "Sort of a sixth sense when it comes to danger."

"I don't know how you function like that. All I could think was that my mom would not approve of his language."

"It was blue," Ethan agreed.

"The bluest. It might have veered into violet," Amelia said. They reached his bike. "Hey, Ethan."

"Yes."

"Thanks for that, thank you for protecting me."

"You're a life worth protecting, Amelia. Makes my job a lot easier." He lifted her onto his motorcycle and re-tied her dress. Amelia watching him with a quiet sort of intensity, hoping the moonless night hid most of what she was thinking.

The drive to her apartment seemed shockingly short, and then they were standing in front of her apartment door, trying to find the best way to say goodbye.

"Traditionally, I think I'm supposed to get a birthday kiss," he said.

"I'm seeing someone," she reminded him.

"Birthday tradition, Amelia. I don't even want to know what might happen if that gets broken," he said. Slowly, he reached for her, settling his hands on her hips. She pressed her palms to his chest, stood on her toes, and placed a soft kiss on his cheek.

"A cheek kiss, really?" he said.

She was still in his arms, tantalizingly close to his face. Her thumb smoothed over his bottom lip. "Kisses with you are like potato chips. You tell yourself you're only going to have one little one, and then it's the next day and you've eaten the entire bag. Goodnight and happy birthday, Ethan Becket."

"Goodnight, Amelia Melly," he said. Reluctantly, he opened his arms and let her go. She back stepped out of his embrace until she bumped the door. After one final smile, she turned and went inside. When he was certain she was safe, he turned and made his way downstairs. He'd have to call Ridge and let him know he was right. It was, hands down, the best birthday of his life.

CHAPTER 8

The alarm beeped. Amelia smacked it, sending it skittering off the edge of her bed and onto the floor. *Note to self, should have bought a nightstand instead of that last pair of shoes.* It was the third day that week she'd woken up feeling blah and irritable. The last few months had been a grand, exciting adventure. First she graduated college, then she landed a dream job and moved cross country. After securing her first, grownup apartment, she met Piedmont and began dating him. *Lows always follow highs.* She could hear her mother's warning ringing in her ears and tried to let it soothe her. Of course she was feeling blah; no one could live on adrenaline forever. But for a naturally upbeat optimist, these occasional bouts with the blues almost made her feel panicked. What if she never recovered? What if she slipped into a depression that lasted forever?

I will be bubbly again, she vowed as she dragged herself out of bed and into the shower. It wasn't a hair wash day, and for that she was thankful. She wasn't in the mood for a blowout, a frightening indicator of her mood. Usually she loved doing her hair and makeup, almost as much as she loved doing other people's. It was why she became a stylist, after all—because a fun hobby spiraled into a career. But today she didn't want to spend forty minutes laboriously drying and styling her hair. She still did full makeup because clients at the salon might change their minds and run away if their stylist rolled up looking like she'd just fallen out of bed and put on the closest pair of pants. And, as always, applying makeup had a fortifying effect on her. It wasn't even the way it looked so much as the soothing, familiar routine.

By the time she was ready to leave, she felt more like herself. The blah feeling was a blip, and one she probably needed to embrace. For the last few months, she had been going eighty miles an hour, burning the candle at both ends. Perhaps the yucky feeling was actually her body's way of protecting herself, of telling her to take a step back, to get a little more sleep, to take a night off of charity events with Piedmont and read a book instead. She would listen—bump up her vegetable intake, get some more sleep, practice a little self-care, and all would be well again in a few days.

She opened the door to the hallway and froze, one foot in the air like a startled fawn. On her doorstep was a single yellow rose. Poking her head out, she looked in both directions but saw and heard no one. She knelt, picked up the rose, and inspected it. There was no note, but she assumed Piedmont had made an early morning delivery before work. He started his day at the crack of dawn and, knowing she liked to sleep until the last possible moment, likely wouldn't have wanted to wake her. Since she hadn't yet reached that stage of adulthood where she owned a vase, she stuck the rose in a glass of water, grabbed her bag, and headed out.

It was a five block walk to the Metro, then two stops, followed by another four blocks of walking. Amelia owned a car, but parking in the city was such a nightmare she barely used it. Selling the car altogether was something she'd been contemplating more and more. The only time she used it anymore was to drive to Ridge and Maggie's house in the suburbs, but she could always take the train and ask them to pick her up from the station, a mere three miles from their house. It wasn't a great car, but selling it would give her a few thousand to feather her nest and create more of a buffer between herself and poverty. Maggie and their brother, Darren, were natural savers. Their oldest brother, Johnny, couldn't care less about money, and Amelia had always had to work harder at keeping it than anyone else in the family. There were just so many pretty, interesting things to buy in the world. At the same time, she desperately wanted to make it, to stand on her own two feet and be a grownup. There was no good way to do that if all her money went toward shoes, clothes, makeup, and eating out, as it had in college. As a testament to her newfound discipline, she had recently opened a separate savings account with an automatic monthly withdrawal. Currently she was only putting in a hundred dollars a month, but over time that would add up. And she could always count on her parents and grandparents for some birthday money. She would put that in, too. Or maybe half, after she splurged on one or two things she'd been wanting. Okay, if ten dollars of birthday money went into the new account, at least that was something, right?

Maybe her newfound blah mood had something to do with her upcoming birthday. Not that twenty three was old by any stretch of the imagination. But she couldn't help feeling like she was on the cusp of some sort of monumental change. While still in college, it had been easy to convince herself she was still a kid. She'd been learning, preparing for her life. She'd gone home for holidays and had remained on her parents' health insurance. Now she had a real job and was responsible for everything on her own. It was hard to continue to feel like a kid while railing at the government for taking so many taxes from her check.

Amelia rounded the corner into the posh neighborhood beside hers. It amazed her how things could change so quickly in the city. Her neighborhood was filled with crummy little studios and walkups like hers while here, a mere two blocks away, were lush townhomes and condos with elevators and doormen. One such doorman had become something of a friend because she saw him every day on her walk. Before moving, she had worried the city would feel aggressively large and scary. The trick, she had learned, was to break it down into several microcosms. It wasn't a massive city of millions; it was the neighborhood where she lived, the neighborhood where she worked, the store where she shopped for groceries, the church she visited when she could convince herself to get out of bed in time on Sunday mornings.

"Good morning, Dennis," she called to the doorman a few paces away. He was a pleasant, fatherly sort of man who never failed to put a smile on her face. And today when he turned to greet her was no different, except for the fact as he smiled and called out a greeting, he also extended his hand and offered her a flower, a white carnation.

Amelia stopped short. Was it coincidence she'd received two flowers on the same morning? "Is this from you, Dennis?"

Dennis grinned. "A secret admirer, Miss Amelia," he replied tipping his cap.

Amelia hurried away, flustered and confused. It seemed an awfully romantic thing for Piedmont to do, but she wouldn't put it past him. In fact, the more she thought about it, the more likely she found it, and now her heart beat quickly for another reason. What if he was planning to propose? What if it was some kind of trail and at the end of it he would be waiting with a ring? He had mentioned their future a few times, but in vague terms of "someday." Surely he wasn't ready for that kind of commitment, was he? They had never even said 'I love you' yet.

No, she was being ridiculous. Of course Piedmont wasn't proposing. She had no idea what he was up to, but she could safely rule out any kind of engagement at the end of it.

On the next block, a man was playing a saxophone, his music case open in front of him. Amelia wished she carried cash for times like these, but everything went on her credit card. She searched her pockets, in case she could locate a spare buck or loose change. In the pocket of her sweater, she struck gold and pulled out a dollar to place in the case. The man nodded as she passed and, without seeming to break stride, handed her a flower. Amelia stopped short and looked at the man, but it was impossible to read his eyes because he was wearing sunglasses. He resumed playing the saxophone as if there had been no interruption, and Amelia continued to walk, hurrying now so as not to miss her train.

She slipped between the Metro doors as they were beginning to close, sat down, and tried to calm her breathing. The cheerful flowers clasped in her hand drew several smiles from the people around her. She smiled in return, though in a dazed sort of way. The middle aged woman beside her seemed especially taken with them until at last she scooted closer and spoke.

"Pretty flowers."

"Thank you," Amelia replied.

"Are they for someone or from someone?" the woman asked.

"They're from someone," Amelia said.

"Ah, a boyfriend?" the woman guessed.

"I think so," Amelia said slowly. She couldn't imagine Piedmont taking the time or energy to set up a delivery by two random strangers, but who else would do such a thing? Her sister was creative and sneaky enough to do it, but if she did, it wouldn't be flowers. It would be croissants or muffins or some other baked good they shared a mutual and fawning love for. For a second, her mind wandered, dreaming of the possibilities of receiving a bouquet of chocolate croissants.

"There's my stop," the woman said, drawing Amelia's attention back to the present. She stood, put her hand in her coat, and handed Amelia a flower. "Have a good day, Amelia."

Amelia was too stunned to even say thank you. She stared at the woman's retreating backside, mouth agape. What in the world of big city mass transit was going on?

She was so dazed she almost missed her stop and had to bolt for the doors, once again narrowly missing being smashed between them. The station was its usual mob, a swarming mass of humanity that varied between commuters and panhandlers. When Amelia first arrived in the city, she had been devastated by the homelessness and need of so many street people. Now, after so many months in the city, she was beginning to feel immune, and that worried her. How did one see so much suffering on a daily basis and not become immune? It was a question she still hadn't answered, and the lack of clarity confused her.

Take it as a sign you're becoming an actual adult, Amelia, Maggie had said when they talked about it. *When you're a kid, everything has a clear answer. Homelessness and poverty seem easy to solve. But when you're an adult you see all the shades of gray. Numbness and cynicism are two different things. You can't walk around with a bleeding heart all day long. You have to do what you can, where you are.*

I'm a stylist who charges two hundred dollars for a haircut, Amelia said.

That's how Mother Theresa got started, Maggie replied, ending the conversation in laughter with no resolution.

Now Amelia's usual sense of throbbing guilt returned as she passed a half dozen panhandlers in various states of distress, their signs and cups compelling her to give money she didn't have. One of them had a dog, adding an extra layer of heartbreak.

Usually they sat passively by and didn't approach, but as Amelia reached the end of the line, one of the men stood and began making a beeline for her, his cup held out in front of him. Her brother-in-law had tried to tell her not to make eye contact—*They can spot a sucker a mile away, and you have the kind of face that says you'll open your purse for them*—but it was too late. She had already locked eyes with the man and seemed unable to sidestep him.

"Got a dollar, lady?" he asked, his voice gruff but his face kind.

Amelia checked her pockets once more to be sure before answering. "Sorry, I gave my last dollar to the saxophone guy."

"Saxophone guys get all the loot," he grumbled and then withdrew the hand behind his back and handed her a flower.

"What is going on?" she asked his retreating backside, but he didn't answer and, even though she was watching him, she somehow lost sight of him in the pulsing crowd.

"What is happening?" she exclaimed to no one in particular, startling an old woman beside her so badly she smacked Amelia on the arm with her newspaper. Wincing, Amelia made a beeline for work, feeling almost paranoid and suspicious of everyone she encountered, wondering if they were going to hand her a flower.

She emerged from the Metro station and bypassed her favorite bakery, almost shading her eyes as she went by. When she first started her job, stopping at the bakery had been a fun part of her routine. But the daily pastries and coffees were putting a major dent in her efforts to be a responsible adult, the kind who has enough money in the bank for emergencies. The kind who realizes croissant and latte cravings do not count as emergencies.

The owner of the bakery knocked on the window and Amelia stopped short, causing the person behind her to also stop short and yell, "Hey, watch it." She moved closer to the window and pressed her face to the glass. The owner beckoned her inside. Amelia pointed to her chest. He nodded. *Yes, you.*

Tentatively, she opened the door and stepped inside. The smell of warm sugar and butter filled her nostrils, reminding her of exactly what her attempt at financial discipline was costing her.

"Amelia, I haven't seen you in two weeks," the baker, Michael, commented.

"I know, and it's been miserable. But I've been trying to be good. You have no idea how many times I've almost broken and bought out your entire supply," Amelia said.

"Your sister's done that twice," Michael said. Maggie was the one who had introduced her to the shop. She had an eye for those sorts of things.

"I'm sorry," Amelia replied, feeling she owed him an apology of some kind, although he probably wasn't going to go under without her six dollar daily habit.

"You'll come back when you can," Michael said, waving her apology away. "But today I have something for you."

Amelia tensed. "You do?"

He nodded and lifted a plate onto the counter. It held a croissant, cut into four pieces. "I tried putting hazelnut spread in the croissants this morning, and I need an expert opinion. Care for a sample?"

"Do squirrels fly? You know I do," she said, eagerly reaching for a sample.

"*Do* squirrels fly?" he asked, tilting his head at her in question.

"I have no idea. It's something my mother says. She's from the south and she says a lot of things none of us can figure out. We've learned to nod and smile a lot," Amelia explained, downing the croissant and resisting the desire to lick her fingers. "That was amazing, I mean, true inspiration. I think you might be on to something here. Best-seller status, for sure."

"So that's a yes then," he said, smiling.

"That's a for the sake of humanity never stop making them," she said, and he laughed.

"Thanks."

"No, thank you," she said. She gathered her flowers and turned to go, but he hailed her back.

"Oh, one more thing."

She turned to him, dearly hoping for more croissant, when he handed her a flower. "You sneaky devil. Were the croissants a ploy?"

"Yes, but after your over-the-top support, I'm going to make some more, see if they sell," he said.

"I don't suppose you're going to tell me who set this up?" she asked, holding her flower aloft.

"I think you'll find out soon enough," he said.

"Cryptic, Michael," she said, shaking her head.

He laughed. "See you."

She wanted to tell him she'd be back after she reached her first savings milestone, that his pastries and coffee and friendly service would be the one splurge she'd allow, at least for one day. But she could only imagine his expression if she unloaded so many personal details on him. So she merely smiled and waved, picking up the pace even more to make it to work on time.

The best part of Amelia's walk was the dog park. She was from a family of dog lovers and had always envisioned herself immediately getting a puppy upon graduation. But of course that was when she was still a kid, six months ago. Now she understood not every apartment allowed animals—hers didn't. And even if she could miraculously find an apartment in her price range that did, she'd have to pay more for a monthly pet allowance. Then there was the monthly cost of ownership—food, vet bills, possibly even a dog sitter to check in on the days Amelia worked long hours and couldn't get home. Plus she'd have to take the dog out, first thing in the morning, late at night, as soon as she got home from work after being on her feet for ten hours. Much as she hated to admit it, she wasn't ready for a dog. She would content herself living vicariously through Maggie's new puppy, the same way she would probably someday content herself with being an aunt until she was ready for children of her own.

The farther she delved into adulthood, the more she realized it wasn't as fun and shiny as she'd always hoped it would be, her finances and the lack of a dog being her biggest struggles at the moment. But the dog park never failed to bring a smile or brighten her day. When she had time, she paused by the gate and watched all the dogs frolic happily with their owners. If she was lucky, someone would take pity on her, or possibly a dog would sense her need, and she'd get the chance to pet a few furry heads, scratch a few ears. Those days were the best, even though she often feared she was turning into a creepy dog stalker. She hadn't yet reached the stage of dog desperation where she carried treats in her pocket and tried to lure strays into her car, but the longer she went without a dog, the closer she got.

But today she had no time to linger by the gate and hope for a pity cuddle. Today she would barely make it on time, thanks to the string of unprecedented flower deliveries. So she hurried past the park, not intending to stop, when she heard little paws scraping behind her. She turned to look and saw a dog, a red rose dangling from its mouth.

"Seriously?" she said, kneeling to take the rose and pat the dog. The dog had other ideas and tackled her, bowling her backwards so she sprawled on her back, all the flowers scattering askew on the sidewalk, along with her purse.

"Are you okay?" a man said, coming to peer over her.

"I'm fine."

"Sorry, he gets a little too enthusiastic sometimes," he said.

"Totally worth it," Amelia told him as he helped her up and stooped to gather her flowers and purse and hand them back to her. By this time she was so frazzled she almost forgot where she was going. Her legs began heading for the salon before the rest of her caught up, the power of muscle memory.

"Your nine o'clock is here and waiting on you," Julie hissed as soon as she opened the door.

"What? No, it's supposed to be a nine thirty," Amelia replied.

"*Nine*," Julie mouthed, shaking her head.

Great, just great. Now Amelia would have no time to put her purse in her locker, fill her water bottle, settle her station, and review the upcoming appointment to learn what she could about the client. Her day was turning into a roller coaster—blah, then surprising, then amazing, then hectic, and now frustrating.

"I'm so sorry I'm late," Amelia said as she approached her station, sounding as frazzled as she felt. "You wouldn't believe the morning I've had."

"Try me," Ethan said, turning in her chair to face her.

"Oh, it was you," she blurted.

"Your money was on the boyfriend?" he guessed.

"A little bit," she confirmed.

"That was probably a safe bet," he said. "You look like you could use this." He presented her with a vase filed with water.

"Do you always carry vases of water for unsuspecting women?" she asked, gently depositing each flower lovingly in the water.

"I live my life by a certain code—to protect flowers and keep them from dying," he said.

"This was sweet and thoughtful and amazing and, some might say, romantic," she said.

"You sounded not quite yourself last time we talked. I thought you could use a pick-me up," he said.

"How? How did you do it?" she asked.

"I called in a few favors, some people I've worked with in the past who are always up for a bit of fun," he said.

"And the dog?"

"We were on the same SEAL team before he got transferred," Ethan said.

"You indexing guys are a laugh riot," she said, smiling.

"Indexing is a high-stress job. We like to unwind on our downtime," he said.

"Speaking of work, I thought you were leaving the country today," she said.

"I'm heading to the airport in," he grasped her hand and drew it closer, checking her watch. "Ninety minutes."

"Is your watch broken?" she asked as he maintained his hold on her hand.

"It's set to military time. So confusing," he said. By taking her hand, he had inadvertently, or maybe not so inadvertently, moved her closer to the chair until she was right in front of him, their legs touching.

"So," she said, resisting the urge to slide her arms around his shoulders by reminding herself they were most likely being watched by all of her coworkers and possibly their clients, too.

"So," Ethan repeated. "I'm here for that consult."

"Consult," she repeated, confused.

"Someone told me I'm going gray and need to have my hair colored," he said. "I thought it best to get a professional opinion."

"Let me take a look here," she said, and now she did lean forward, sifting her fingers gently through his hair. "Hmm, it looks pretty good to me. How old are you?"

"Twenty eight," he whispered.

"That's pretty old, but you're in luck. I think you're going to be able to keep your natural color," she said. "Unless maybe you'd prefer the gray?"

"I've been told I have the coloring for it," he said.

"You do have excellent coloring. Very, uh, healthy," she said.

"It's probably a good thing I don't need anything done. I was browsing a brochure while I was waiting, and I don't think I could afford you," he said.

"Maybe we could make some sort of exchange. I could do your hair, and you could index things for me," she suggested.

"I don't come cheap either," he said.

"Yeah? What's a good indexer go for these days?" she asked.

"I could tell you, but then I'd have to kill you," he said. The heat from his gaze was so intense, it left her a little breathless.

"You left me nowhere to go from there," she said.

He laughed. "I should go anyway. I have a flight to catch."

"Have fun in 'Canada'."

"I'll try," he promised.

"Wear sunscreen. Last time you came home with a pink nose."

"You know how brutal that Canadian sun can be," he said. "Are you going to walk me outside?"

Danger, danger, danger. If she walked him outside, she'd be in his arms and kissing him like an ant on tree sap. "I have a client in a few minutes," she said, clearing her throat when it came out all raspy.

"I guess this is goodbye then. I'll see you sometime after I get back."

"Hey, thanks for making my day and possibly my year," she said.

"Only a year? Guess I'll have to try harder next time." He kissed the tip of his finger and touched it to her cheek before standing and making his way out of the salon. Amelia could swear it wasn't her imagination all eyes were on him.

"Who was that?" Her client had arrived and was now standing beside her watching Ethan walk out of the shop, along with everybody else. Amelia hadn't filled her water or put her purse away, but she found she didn't so much care anymore.

"A friend," Amelia said.

"Have mercy, is he available?" the woman asked.

"For your granddaughter?" Amelia asked. Her client was seventy two and on the last visit told Amelia she had a granddaughter about her age.

"Child, you don't waste a man like that on someone who doesn't know what to do with him, and it's been a while since I had a pet," the woman mused.

Amelia tried to imagine Ethan's reaction to the disconcerting conversation. "He's not exactly the kind of man who likes to be kept."

"I suppose that's why we like that kind," the woman replied, sighing. "They're like tropical birds, attractive but best left in their natural habitat."

It was amazing to Amelia the woman could capture Ethan's essence after merely a glimpse: he was beautiful but wild and uncontained.

CHAPTER 9

Lately Ethan's life had been nothing but work. It seemed as if every terror cell in the world had pooled their resources and decided to act in one capacity or another. In three weeks he went to eight different countries on assignment. His social life was at a virtual standstill. He had no time and energy for friends, let alone dating. Though lately he didn't much have the heart for the game he had once loved. Maybe he was getting too old for it. Recently it seemed like when saw a pretty woman who gave him all the right signals, he couldn't seem to make himself engage. What he wanted most at the end of a long workweek was sleep and then coffee and then more sleep. He was beginning to understand why Ridge had transitioned away from being a field agent. How long could he reasonably keep up with the demands of his job? He wasn't yet thirty, and he was exhausted.

He had always loved his job, first in the navy, then as a SEAL, and now as an undercover agent. He thrived on adventure, on taking chances, on doing things few other people in the world could do. But lately the job had lost its shine. Who cared that he was on an elite task force when he had no one to tell? Even his family back home in Vermont had no idea what he did. Ridge and Maggie were lucky they worked together and could share the stress of their job. They didn't have to keep secrets. Ethan realized the direction of his thoughts and groaned. Just a few months ago he had been making fun of Ridge at his wedding, and now he was beginning to envy him. It wasn't that he was ready to settle down, per se, more that he was ready for someone to share things with, to unload the burden a little, to not feel so alone in the world. When he was in the SEALs, they were his brothers. They still were, but most of them had wives now. Some of them had kids. It wasn't the same as it had been; they weren't a team anymore. They were friends, busy friends who rarely had the time or energy to get together anymore.

Now it was Saturday, his first weekend off in a month and his first morning home after a whirlwind trip to Somalia. He sat at his tiny table in his tiny apartment, trying not to wonder if this was all there was to life: work, sleep, repeat, wake up alone, go to bed alone, repeat, repeat, repeat. It had seemingly been forever since he'd gone on a date, even longer since he'd attempted an actual girlfriend. He had always insisted he wasn't boyfriend material, but lately he was beginning to rethink things. What would it be like to be in an actual relationship? Would he get tired of being with the same person, as he feared he might? Or would it be nice to have the security of knowing someone, of digging deep and delving into secrets? What would happen when they got over the surface stuff and hit flaws? Could he be with someone messy? Could someone be with him with all his emotional baggage and liabilities?

A newspaper lay open in front of him, and it was doubtless why he was feeling so morose this morning. A picture of Amelia blared out from the society section, ensconced on the arm of Piedmont Bonvoy at some charity event. She looked radiant, as if she belonged to high society and all the trappings that went with it. Bonvoy was looking at her like she was his every dream come true, and she probably was. Ethan didn't even normally read the paper, but he had glimpsed it in the airport yesterday, had glimpsed Amelia, and plunked down the money for it before he even realized what he was doing. He hadn't talked to her in weeks. Had she thought about him? Probably not. She was too busy living it up with her famous lawyer boyfriend. He was officially her boyfriend now. Ethan knew because the magazine article described her as the "Serious girlfriend of Piedmont Bonvoy." Serious? When had that come about? Last Ethan knew, they were keeping it casual. Of course that had been weeks ago, before he became busy settling the world's problems on another continent while Bonvoy stayed home and argued over money in court, nice and cozy. Not that Ethan was bitter.

He tossed the paper away and sipped his coffee. A loud knock rapped on the door, and he jumped, sloshing coffee on the paper and table. "Great, now I'm turning into a nervous old lady," he muttered, using a napkin to wipe up the coffee before it could spread.

For one wild, hopeful second, he thought maybe it was Amelia come to catch up. She knew he'd been busy with work because he told her he'd be occupied with a big project. He didn't think for a minute she believed he worked in the private sector, but she'd never called him on the lie, and for that he was grateful. They had been well on their way to becoming good friends before he left, texting most days and talking on the phone occasionally on others. And now he hadn't spoken to her in six weeks. Six weeks, three days, and fourteen hours, to be exact.

But it wasn't Amelia at the door. "Officers, what can I do for you?" he asked, mentally running through the list of why two units were at his door. He had done a lot of things the local police would consider illegal but were allowed by his job and federal law. It was complex. Usually the police looked the other way and pretended they didn't know what the feds were up to when they skirted in and out of places they shouldn't be with unseen weapons. But occasionally one of the locals got something in his craw and it came to a head. Of course that was only if they got caught, which Ethan hadn't been. The only weapon currently in his possession was his service pistol.

The two officers stood on the doorstep serious and unsmiling. One of them assessed Ethan while the other let his eyes roam around the interior of the apartment. Ethan shifted his weight, blocking the view on principal. "We've had a complaint," the first officer said, the one who didn't have roaming eyes.

"What kind of complaint?" Ethan asked. It couldn't be a noise complaint because he hadn't been home for weeks.

"Stalking," the first officer answered.

"What?" Ethan said, frowning. "What are you talking about?"

"We've had a complaint, a serious and credible complaint, that you've been stalking and harassing a woman," the officer said.

"What woman?" Ethan asked.

"Amelia Eldridge," the first officer said, and Ethan started to laugh.

"What are you guys, like rent a cops? Okay, she got me, I'm a stalker." He put up his hands in surrender and, quick as a wink, the second cop cuffed him.

"You think this is funny?" the first cop said.

"Yeah, I think this is a joke," Ethan said. "Is Amelia out there?" He tried to glance behind them, but the cop who had cuffed him slammed him against the wall.

"Don't move," he growled.

"Hey, whoa, wait a minute. You guys are going a little far here," Ethan said. "Did Amelia set this up or not?"

"We haven't spoken with the victim. The complainant was her boyfriend."

Ethan blinked in rapid succession a few times. Did Bonvoy set this up? Or was it real? Amelia's boyfriend might actually have a beef with him, if he knew about their fledgling friendship. Was he the sort of man who would take out the competition by any means necessary?

"I have never stalked a woman in my life. I'm sure Amelia would tell you the same thing, if you asked her." It was better to play along, on the off chance these guys were legit.

"Do you mind if we take a look around?" the first cop asked.

"Yes, I very much do," Ethan said.

"Too bad, we have a warrant."

"I want to see it, and some ID," Ethan demanded. The cops pulled out their badges and held the warrant aloft for him to inspect. If they were forgeries, they were exact replicas. "Fine, take a look around."

"Oh, thanks for the permission," the second cop said sarcastically, tucking the warrant back in his pocket. He made his way into the bedroom while the first cop stayed with Ethan, letting his eyes roam over the interior of the apartment. Ethan had no idea what they were hoping or expecting to find.

"You going to let me out of these cuffs?" he asked.

"Not until we're satisfied there's nothing to see here," the first cop said. Ethan tried hard to keep a cap on his temper. He wasn't accustomed to being treated so by guys who were supposedly on the same team. When this was over and everything had been sorted out, he would let them know his opinions on the matter, in no uncertain terms. Until then, cooperation was his best option.

"Larry, you gotta see this," the cop who was in his bedroom called. Larry went into the bedroom, tugging Ethan along beside him. They entered the room and stopped short.

"Whoa," Larry said. Before them was a massive poster on the wall, cutout pictures of Amelia covering it completely. Below that was a half-burned candle and a letter made out of magazine cutouts. Ethan couldn't read it, but it seemed to be some kind of plea or threat.

"Okay then," Larry drawled. When he was finally able to tear his eyes off the picture, he turned to Ethan. "You have the right to remain silent. Anything you say can or will…"

"You're mirandizing me? What for?" Ethan demanded.

"Stalking, terrorizing, threatening, you name it," the second cop said.

"But I've never seen that before," Ethan said. His patience was at an end. He twisted out of the first cop's grasp and saw them both place a hand on their weapons.

"I think we're going to need some backup," the second cop said.

"For sure," the first cop agreed.

"Wait, what?" Ethan demanded, spinning in a circle to try and face both of them. "What is going on?"

"Backup," the first cop yelled, and now Ethan spun toward the doorway in time to see Amelia enter in a too-big cop uniform.

"You called?" she said, hanging onto the doorpost and leaning into the room.

"We're going to need some help with this one," the first cop, "Larry" said.

"I think I've got it from here, guys. Thanks so much." She patted their backs as they left the room and filed past her. Ethan watched in silence as she made her way into the room and stared at the poster of her.

"Ethan, this is a sickness. You need help," she said.

"I'm pretty sure you're the one who needs help, and I'm positive you're going to need it after I get these cuffs off," he said.

"Oh, shoot, I forgot to get the key from them," Amelia said, giving him a devilish grin.

"You think I need a key to get out of cuffs?" he asked.

"I don't know. Do you?" she asked.

He got out of the cuffs and placed them in her upturned palm.

"Hmm, what an interesting skill for a regional representative of an indexing firm to possess," she said.

He made no reply.

"How was your trip to 'Canada'?"

"It was 'good'," he said, mimicking her air quotes. "It would seem as though you missed me."

"What makes you say that?" she asked.

"A hunch," he said. "I saw your picture in the paper."

He couldn't be sure, but she seemed to blush. "Oh, that."

"Yes, that."

There was an awkward lull. "I should probably go," she said. She took a step away, but he caught her hand.

"Don't go." He swallowed and let go of her hand. "We have a lot of catching up to do. Friend stuff."

"I did bring breakfast," she admitted sheepishly.

"It's my favorite meal of the day," he said.

"Maybe you can tell me about Canada, in the vaguest possible terms," she said.

"It was surprisingly hot, almost like I was at the equator," he said.

"Funny how that seems to happen a lot in your line of work," she said. They shared a smile and she snapped to attention. "Breakfast."

"Right, breakfast," he agreed. He motioned for her to walk in front of him and brewed a fresh pot of coffee when they arrived at the kitchen. Amelia set out the pastries and breakfast sandwiches she'd brought, enough to feed a half dozen more people.

"That's a lot of food," he noted.

"Better to have too much than not enough," she returned. They sat and filled their plates, waiting for the coffee to finish. "How was your trip, really?"

"Exhausting," he said.

"International travel is probably not as glamorous as I imagine," she said.

"Not the way I do it," he said.

"You look tired," she said.

"Thank you?"

"I meant that in a concerned way, not a put down. Are you doing all right?" Her feet searched for a place to land on the tall uncomfortable bar stools that served as his dining chairs. He should really invest in some grownup, quality furniture one of these days. He took her feet and settled them in his lap, leaving his hand to rest lightly on her ankle.

"I'm doing all right," he told her.

"Ethan," she pressed.

He sighed. "It's...I don't know."

"Stressful?" she guessed.

"Yes, but not in the way that you might think. When I was in the SEALs, it was stressful, but like 'save the person' stressful or 'do the thing before the bomb blows up' stressful. The new job is 'do the thing for vague reasons and then get yelled at by a committee' stressful."

"You can quit and find a new job. With your skills, any indexing firm would be happy to have you," she said.

"This is the path you're supposed to follow when you leave the SEALs. Otherwise, why go?" he said.

"Who says? Make your own path. What's your end game? What do you want to do? If you could do anything in the world, what would it be?"

"Coach football," he blurted without thinking. "But not really. I mean, nobody does that for a living, do they?"

"Actually, a lot of people do," she said.

"But I was a Navy SEAL. I worked unbelievably hard to get that position, and then I left it for a presumably better position. How crazy would it be to leave my current job to coach high school football?"

"What's wrong with crazy? Do you know what my degree is in?" she asked.

He shook his head.

"Actuarial science. I spent four years training to take on one of the highest paying jobs in the country. I took math courses that would bore you on name alone, dozens of them. I had five job offers at the start of my junior year. And then I walked away to color and blow dry hair for a living. But, guess what, I love doing hair and makeup. It brings me joy to help bring out the best in other people."

"So you're, like, crazy smart, in addition to everything else," he surmised.

"Yep, I'm the total package," she said, stealing a bite of his half-finished croissant.

"Hey, don't poach my food," he complained, reaching for her too-sweet coffee. He took his black, but occasionally he liked it loaded with cream and sugar, as hers was now. He drained her coffee and sat back. "What?" he asked when she continued to stare at him.

"It doesn't bother you to share food and drinks?" she asked.

"Should it? Do you have cooties?" he asked.

She nodded, and for some reason the moment turned tense and serious. Ethan's eyes fell to her lips. He could remember how they felt on his down to the minutest detail, and he was shocked to realize she was the last person he'd kissed. How had he gone so long without a date? Amelia's feel and smell and even her taste seemed permanently imprinted on him, but how could he expect anything else when he had basically been living a monastic existence?

"Ethan," she whispered. With effort, he pulled his gaze from her lips back up to her eyes. "Tell me why you want to coach football."

The question took a few seconds to register. He swallowed hard and tried to focus. "I didn't have the best family life, growing up. Football was my salvation, my ticket out. When I was on the field, everything was okay. My coach became like a father to me. It was he who encouraged me to do well, on and off the field, he who made sure my grades were up to snuff, and he who encouraged me into the navy, even into the SEALs. I'd like to think I could one day have that sort of impact on someone."

"I'm sure you will, at least on your own children," she said.

"I'm not sure I ever want kids," he said.

"Why not?" she asked.

"Because I didn't have the best example. I don't want to be a screwed up dad."

"But you said you did have a good example in your coach. And I think to be a screwed up dad, you'd have to be a screwed up man to begin with. You're not a screwup. You're a noble man of good character," she said.

"A noble man of good character," he repeated. "I have never heard anyone talk that way in real life." Despite the scoffing, he was pleased by her words. "Is Piedmont Bonvoy a noble man of good character?"

"Do you think I would date anyone who wasn't?" she countered.

"I don't think you should. Whether you would is another story. Sometimes women do unimaginable things. Sometimes they date total losers, men who take them for granted, who use and abuse them."

"I know my worth, and I'm not willing to settle," she assured him.

"I'm glad to hear that, Amelia, because if I thought he was mistreating you..." he trailed off, leaving the rest unspoken.

"What?" she prompted.

What would he do if he thought someone was hurting her? He searched his mental inventory as he stared at her and she watched him, awaiting an answer. "I'd probably kill him."

She shuddered. "Don't joke like that."

"What makes you think I'm joking? There aren't a lot of people I genuinely care about. For those I do, I'd go to any lengths to protect and keep them safe."

"You worry me sometimes, Ethan Becket."

"I worry myself sometimes, Amelia Melly. Were those real cops?"

"No. Larry's my neighbor. The other guy was his friend from acting class. Blue doctored up the badges and warrant for me. He's really good at forgery. It's amazing how the people who work at my sister's company have so many secret, interesting talents: hacking, forgery, speaking Arabic, training in hand-to-hand combat."

"The corporate world is a jungle," he said. He smiled, but it still looked a little sad.

She rested her hand on his wrist. "Hey, you are loved, you know that, right? You have a whole circle of people who care desperately about you."

He eased his arm backwards, sliding her hand from his wrist to his fingers, lacing them together. "I'm not suicidal, if that's what you're thinking. Just lacking a bit of direction at the moment."

"Sometimes vets have trouble readjusting to civilian life," she said.

"I'm not exactly a civilian," he said.

She quirked an eyebrow at him, and he realized he had just admitted the truth of his job to her, at least in part.

"I mean, working at an indexing firm is kind of like war, you know?" He squeezed her hand.

"I'm onto you," she said.

"Yeah? Tell me what you're onto."

"You keep up this charm offensive to hold everyone at arms length. You try to pretend you don't care about anything, but you care about everything too much. Beneath the tough soldier act, you're a fluffy marshmallow. I bet you love babies and puppies."

"Who doesn't love babies and puppies?" he asked.

She opened her mouth to say something and closed it again immediately.

"Piedmont doesn't like babies and puppies," he guessed, smiling in triumph.

"It's not like that. He's a cat person, and he's never been exposed to children, being that he's an only child and basically came out of the birth canal doing complex calculus."

"Is that what you guys have in common? Your deep love of math?" Ethan said.

"Yes, we share a passionate love of math," she said, her temper flaring.

Ethan's smile fled. "Gross, Amelia. I don't actually want to know what goes on between you two."

"Then don't ask," she snapped.

"Do you love him, really?" he asked.

She looked away. "I haven't said the words yet, but it's heading there."

"And where do I fit into that equation?" he wondered.

"We're friends. We already established that," she reminded him.

"And will we still be friends if you and he get married?" he asked. His hand trailed lightly over her ankle.

"Everyone's relationships change after marriage. I've barely seen Maggie, and she's my sister," Amelia said.

"You're sidestepping. You know as well as I do he wouldn't like it if he knew you were here right now, that he wouldn't like it if he knew we were friends."

"That's not true, he's not the jealous type," she said.

"If he's male and breathing, he's the jealous type." She shook her head. "Does he know you're here? Does he know we text and call?"

She shook her head again.

He sat back with a smile of triumph. Amelia sat up, removing her legs from his lap. "Don't make me feel guilty. Nothing has happened between us. I haven't once cheated on Piedmont. You and I are friends, nothing more."

"Nothing has happened between us. You haven't once cheated on Piedmont. You and I are friends, but there's something more. You know it, and I know it, so let's do ourselves a favor and not pretend it's not there when we both feel it."

She stood and began collecting things into her basket. "You have a high opinion of yourself."

"I know my worth, and I'm not willing to settle," he said.

"Good, great, awesome," she said, tossing items pell-mell into the basket in her haste to get away.

"You seem awfully uptight for someone who's doing nothing wrong," he noted, amused.

She paused to glare at him. "Don't tease me about this."

"Why not?"

"Because you make me feel like I'm doing something wrong," she said.

"Maybe you are, but not the way you think," he said.

"Huh?" she asked.

"Maybe he's not the one you're hurting because he's not the one you're supposed to be with," he suggested.

"We've been over this, Ethan," she said.

"Have we?"

"Yes. You want me because you can't have me, because I'm with Piedmont. If I were available, you'd..." she broke off and shook her head.

"I'd what?" he prompted.

"You tell me. And be honest, for both our sakes."

He took a breath and reached for her hand again, clasping it and holding it against his rapidly thumping heart. "If you were available, maybe I would realize you're the best thing that's ever come along. Maybe I'd fall for you, so deep and so hard I wouldn't realize other women exist anymore. Maybe I would get my act together and be ready to be the kind of man you need me to be."

"Maybe," she repeated sadly. "You want me to upend my life for maybe, but I can't, and I won't. And so we're friends. The end."

He released a pent up breath of frustration. "Don't you realize how far I've come to get to where we are now?"

"Yes, I very much do. But I'm afraid I need all the way or nothing at all." She wanted to hug him. He could read it in her expression. Her arms lifted and then she forced them down again because she was afraid. She was afraid if she hugged him, it wouldn't be enough, that she would lose control and give in to him completely. He admired her self-control because he was lacking it altogether.

"You should go now," he said. It was all he could do to release her hand and watch her walk away, which she did without needing to be told twice. Before she shut the door, she turned and gave him one sad, little smile, and she was gone.

CHAPTER 10

A week later, Maggie and Ridge hosted a party at the common room of their housing development. The rental also included the pool for the day, good news for Ridge's former navy buddies who loved nothing better than being in the water.

"If a SEAL goes too long without a swim, his skin dries up and falls off, or so the legend goes," Jordan told Amelia as they sat poolside with Jordan's new baby. Amelia spent a long time holding him, giving Jordan a break so she could eat. It was also a handy way to soak up baby time. Between that and Ridge and Maggie's new puppy, she was in heaven.

Unfortunately for Amelia, Jordan and Shimmer didn't stay long. "There's no tired like new baby tired," Jordan told her.

"If you ever need a break, please give me a call. Seriously, I could hold him all day," Amelia said.

"I may take you up on that. Having a new baby and being away from family is no joke," Jordan said, her lip quivering with unshed tears.

"I'm off work in two days. I'll come over and you can nap or read or do whatever you want to do," Amelia promised her.

"I'll be looking forward to it," Jordan said, hugging her goodbye.

When she was gone, Ethan emerged from the water and stood over Amelia.

"If I didn't know better, I might think you're avoiding me," he said.

"I'm not avoiding you; I'm avoiding the water," she said.

"Why?"

She pointed to her head. "Brazilian blowouts and chlorine don't mix."

He squinted. "What gibberish are you speaking, lady? Are you trying to tell me you're so fussy you don't want to get your hair wet?"

"Not wet, *chlorinated*. What part of Brazilian blowout do you not understand?"

"All of it," he said. He reached down, plucked her phone from her fingers, set it aside, and scooped her into his arms.

"Ethan, don't."

"Yep," he replied as he carried her to the water and jumped in.

"Ugh, boys," she said when she emerged.

"What is the big deal about your hair? It always looks amazing," he said.

"It's supposed to. It's sort of my calling card, and you are not helping at this moment." She tried to swim away from him, but he pulled her back.

"Amelia, your hair could turn puce and fall out, and you'd still be the most beautiful woman I know," he said sincerely.

She blew out a breath. "You're making it really hard for me to maintain my irritation at you."

"That's sort of my calling card. I frustrate people to the point of murder and then charm them into loving me again," he said.

"You're super good at it," she said. Still, she turned and headed for the side of the pool.

He grasped her hand and pulled her back again. "Why do you keep trying to get away from me?"

"Why do you assume everything is about you? I'm merely trying to stay alive here. We're in the deep end, and I can't tread water forever." The pool was deep, eight feet where they were swimming

"I can," he said and fastened her arms around his neck, holding them both afloat while he kicked.

"This is intimate," she noted, but it wasn't necessarily a complaint.

"This is nostalgic. I used to have to tread for hours," he said.

"You miss being in the SEALs," she said.

"Sometimes. I miss being a part of something, of being on a team."

"You still have them," she pointed out, gazing around the pool. "Theoretically," she added when she realized they were alone. "Where did everyone go?"

"To see the new puppy," he said. "You must have missed my text this week because you didn't reply."

"Our last conversation made me reevaluate a few things."

"Me, for instance," he said.

"No, our friendship. If I'm going to make a go of things with Piedmont, I need to prioritize."

"So that's it, we're done?"

"Of course not. We're still friends," she assured him.

"Can we text and call?" he asked.

"Sure."

"But we can't get together and grab coffee," he clarified.

"Friends can get together for coffee," she said.

"So, what can't we do?" he asked.

"Namely this," she said as they swayed gently in the water, her arms around his neck, his hands on her waist.

"Swimming?" he guessed.

"You know what I'm talking about. The touching, the intimacy. The almost moments."

"How does one stop an almost moment?" he asked.

"One never lets it begin in the first place," she said.

"Hmm, I see. So when does this new order start?" he asked.

"As soon as I can touch bottom and am no longer in fear of drowning," she said.

"Let's move this conversation to the ocean," he replied.

She laughed. "I have to go dry off. Piedmont's stopping by whenever he can get off work."

"You mean he could walk in here any minute?" Ethan replied, his grasp on her waist tightening.

"This is the very definition of not helping," she said.

"It's your rule, not mine. If it were up to me, we'd roll all those almost moments into a big, cataclysmic life event," he said.

"You're so ridiculously charming it's nearly irresistible," she said.

"Nearly's not a good word in this context," he said.

"It ranks up there with maybe," she said.

"You're the comeback queen."

"I was a math major. For survival's sake, it was imperative I also be cute and witty," she said.

The door to the common room opened and someone stepped out. Amelia swam to the ladder and exited the pool, bypassing her brother-in-law, Ridge, as she made her way inside. Ridge remained by the pool surveying Ethan for a moment before bringing two fingers to his eyes and pointing them at Ethan in the universal, *I'm watching you,* gesture.

Ethan drew an imaginary circle around his head, a halo.

Ridge held up horns behind his own head and smashed his fist into his palm.

"Are you trying to tell me you're a Satanist now?" Ethan asked.

"Pretty sure you get what I'm trying to say," Ridge said. "She's twenty three; she's a baby."

"You know I'm only twenty eight," Ethan said. "Not exactly Father Time."

"You ceased to be a child on your first mission," Ridge said, reminding him of all he'd seen and done. "She's an innocent, a civilian who has no idea how far we've gone in our jobs."

"She's more mature than you realize," Ethan said.

"Are you?" Ridge asked. "I've seen what you do to women. I don't want that to happen to Amelia."

"You're really getting into the big brother thing," Ethan said, aiming for a lighter tone.

"I'm not joking, Ethan. This is my wife's beloved little sister. I love you like a brother, but you hurt her, and we're through."

"You're in luck; I'm not the one she wants," Ethan said.

Ridge's eyes narrowed on him, morphing from anger to concern in a heartbeat. He was looking at him the same way he used to after a particularly difficult mission. "You doing okay, Beck?"

"What's okay in our world, Cam?" Ethan asked. He took a deep dive and didn't come up for a long time, until he thought his lungs might burst. When he emerged, Amelia was sitting on the side of the pool, wearing the same look of concern Ridge had used a few minutes ago.

"You were down a long time. I was starting to worry," she said.

"I can hold my breath for a long time," he reminded her.

"It felt long from up here," she said.

"It's supposed to," he said.

"I'm leaving," she said.

"I'll walk you out." He slipped out of the pool and she handed him a towel.

"I'm watching Shimmer and Jordan's baby in a couple of days so she can get a break. I thought maybe you could pick up dinner and eat with us, thereby saving her the trouble of making a meal."

"Good plan," he said, toweling his hair as they walked. They reached her car, coincidentally parked beside his motorcycle. She leaned on her vehicle while he leaned on his.

"Ethan Becket, Becket Ethan, I hope you understand that my decision to pull back on our relationship has nothing to do with you. It's more of a self-preservation thing."

He was growing weary of the alternating viewpoints that he was either a charity case or an ogre. Sure, he'd broken a few hearts in his past, but he wasn't a monster. He gave a harsh laugh. "I wouldn't exactly call it a relationship, Amelia. I mean, we've had a few laughs and a couple of good kisses, but we barely know each other. I've had a longer and more meaningful relationship with my dry cleaner."

By her wounded expression, he knew he'd cut her. *This is why people think you can't be trusted with women's hearts—because you can't.* Before he could try to make amends, another car pulled up beside them and Piedmont Bonvoy emerged, smiling at Amelia like she was the winning Powerball lottery ticket that was going to change his life forever.

"I made it," he announced, stating the obvious. Ignoring Ethan as if he weren't there, he reached for her and kissed her neck. It was a blatantly possessive gesture that signaled he was possibly more cognizant of Ethan than he let on.

Amelia closed her eyes and hugged him, as if his presence was a relief to her because it provided a reprieve from him, Ethan, and his hurtful comment. "I was just leaving," she said, keeping her eyes closed.

"But I didn't get to see the puppy," Piedmont protested.

"You don't like puppies," she reminded him.

"You do, and I know it's important to you. Besides, it's not like I hate puppies. I'm not psychotic. I just prefer cats. And I was hoping to talk with your sister and brother-in-law."

"Really? After a long day of work you want to spend time with my family?" she asked.

"I want to do anything that matters to you," he said.

Ethan felt like he should be taking notes on, "How to impress a woman and her family," because he was getting a master class in it. "Well, I'm going to take off," he said. Jutting his hand out, he added, "Bonvoy, nice to see you again." Piedmont shook his hand with zero recognition. "Melly, see you Tuesday." He didn't wait around to see the effect of his words or hear Amelia try to explain who he was or why she'd be seeing him again on Tuesday. Instead he got on his bike and drove away, trying hard not to think of anything at all.

CHAPTER 11

I*'ve made a huge mistake.* It was all Ethan could think while his date chattered endlessly over supper. Her voice was like what donkeys must sound like if they could talk—overly loud and braying. *This is what happens when you pick up women at the gym.* She'd seemed so perfect when he'd caught sight of her lifting massive weights beside him. But it turned out she was a health nut who had spent the last forty minutes talking about the amazing benefits of whey and protein powders.

"How about chocolate cupcakes? Do you ever eat those?" he blurted, interrupting a fascinating comparison of peanut butter and almond powders.

"I don't eat refined sugars," she replied, her lip curling in distaste.

"Huh," he said, purposely tearing open a sugar packet and dumping it into his iced tea. His head hurt, and he was exhausted. On a date with Shrek's sidekick was the very last place he wanted to be. Yes, she was very pretty and, yes, she could probably beat him in an arm wrestling contest, but he didn't care. She was fundamentally lacking in...something. Maybe everything.

She's not Amelia, the annoying little voice whispered in the back of his head. It had been doing it all night, hence the headache. He'd tried to make up to Amelia last week at Shimmer's house, but she had been oh-so-polite, distant, and cool. He missed her warmth, her laughter, her orneriness, the way she looked at him with such tenderness that it made his insides ache with longing to be worthy of such emotion. Amelia made him want to be a better man. His date made him want to shove breadsticks in his ears to drown out the sound of her incessant bleating.

When at last the painful meal was over, she suggested they go back to his place. What he wanted to say was that he would invite her into his inner sanctum over his cold dead body. What he said instead was that he had an early morning. He had no desire to kiss her goodnight, but she took the decision out of his hands by standing on her toes and shoving her tongue down his throat in what had to be his grossest, worst kiss since fifth grade when he was still learning how. Even worse was the fact that she tasted like the beets she'd eaten for supper. His mouth felt like he'd licked an anthill.

Once home, he plopped into bed and stared at the ceiling, wishing for sleep. He hadn't been doing much of that the last few days, not since his spat with Amelia. Had it been a spat? That word implied they'd both been at fault, but Amelia had done nothing wrong. It was he who made a cutting remark and hurt her feelings, his usual M/O. He couldn't seem to get close to a woman without pushing her away, not even a friend, as Amelia had been. *Was*, as Amelia still *was*. They were still friends because she had said so. Just because he had created a rift between them didn't mean it had to be permanent. He would charm her out of her hurt; he was good at that.

When his phone rang and he saw her name, he wondered if he was dreaming. Had he conjured her by the power of wanting? Whatever the reason, he wasn't about to waste the call. He pressed the button to connect, but before he could utter a word, he heard her scream.

He sat up. "Amelia?"

"Ethan, help me."

He could hear the sounds of a struggle in the background, and he gripped the phone tighter. "Amelia, I'm really not in the mood for a prank right now."

"Help me, two men are taking me. They're Russian…" she said, and the line went dead. Ethan tried to call her back, but there was no answer. He tapped his fingers on his knee, trying to decide what to do. Obviously she was pranking him again. He shouldn't fall for it. It would teach her a lesson if he refused. But on the teeny, tiny off chance something had actually happened to her, he would never forgive himself.

He came to this decision approximately ten minutes after he holstered his gun, hopped on his bike, and started to drive. Even if it was another prank, which it undoubtedly was, it was a foot in the door, a way to talk to her and make amends.

Traffic was blessedly light as he wound his way to her house, speeding like all demon fire was behind him. He reached for his phone, intending to text Maggie and Ridge to see if they knew what was up, but then he remembered they were in France on assignment and Amelia was watching their new puppy. She'd been incredibly excited about it, had spent a long time talking to Jordan about it on Tuesday as she carefully avoided him.

She didn't answer his buzz when he arrived at her building. No one else would let him in, so he broke in, annoyed at the thirty second delay. He sprinted up the stairs to her apartment. When he saw the puppy wandering aimlessly around the hallway, he knew something was wrong. She would never, ever put Maggie and Ridge's puppy in danger, not even for the best prank in the world.

He pulled out his gun and quickly swept her apartment. Signs of a struggle were apparent. He picked up the dog and pounded on her neighbor's door.

"What?" Larry the fake cop ripped open the door, frowning.

"Amelia's gone. Did you hear anything about thirty minutes ago?"

"Uh," Larry said, scratching his head, blinking in confusion. It was clear Ethan had just woken him. "I heard stuff, I thought it was a different neighbor, the noisy one who screams."

"She screamed?" Ethan pressed.

Larry nodded, his face paling.

"What else, what did you hear, anything at all?"

"Just screaming, bumping, and men speaking words I couldn't understand. It was some other language, something rough."

"Russian," Ethan said, and Larry nodded.

"Probably."

"Here." Ethan shoved the puppy into Larry's unwilling arms. "Watch the dog until either Amelia comes back or her sister, Maggie, comes to get him. His name is Smokey, food's in Amelia's apartment. Lock it up for me."

"Ethan, what is going on?" Larry asked, shoving his head out of his doorway to call to Ethan's retreating backside.

"I have no idea, but I'm going to find out," Ethan said. Panic threatened to creep in, but he pushed it away. His first thought was that she had been taken because of him. Someone somewhere had connected him to her. It was every agent's worst fear, that the job would endanger the people closest to him. But he hadn't worked with the Russians since he was a newbie SEAL. Most of his work since he joined the agency had been in Africa and the Middle East. There were plenty of Russians in Africa, but none connected to him. So he discounted himself from the equation and went to the next logical source.

Piedmont Bonvoy answered the door wearing a fluffy bathrobe, as if he were a ninety-year-old man and Ethan was some type of scout selling magazines door to door.

"Why are you pounding on my door?" Piedmont demanded.

"Do you work with the Russians?" Ethan blurted.

"What? Who are you?"

"Do you work with the Russians?" Ethan repeated, taking a step forward as Piedmont took one back.

"I'm going to call the police," Piedmont said. His hand reached into his robe. Ethan grabbed him by the fluffy lapels and slammed him against the door.

"Just answer the question. Do you work with the Russians?"

"No, I have no Russian clients," Piedmont said, pushing Ethan's hands off him. "What's this about?"

"They took her, they took Amelia," Ethan said. He doubled over and struggled to get a deep breath. If the Russians weren't connected to Piedmont, he might never figure out who took her or where. To his surprise, Piedmont stumbled backwards and did the same thing, his chest meeting his knees, gasping as the air seemed to leave his lungs and his legs failed him.

Ethan straightened. "What do you know, Bonvoy?"

"They sent me a letter, threatening to take her," Piedmont said.

"Who?"

"The Russians," he exclaimed.

"You said they weren't your clients."

"They're not. You think I have thugs and gangsters for clients? They're on the other side, in an all-out war with my clients. They threatened to take Amelia unless I made the case disappear."

Ethan stared at him, speechless. "You put her in danger, and you never said anything?"

"Of course I did. I went straight to the feds. They said the threat wasn't legit, that there was no way they could get to her or take her out of the country."

"Did Amelia know she was in danger?"

Piedmont shook his head, straightening. "I didn't want to worry her. I hired private security to watch her. They were supposed to start tomorrow morning." He bent over again. "What am I going to do, what am I going to do, what am I going to do?" He straightened again. "I have to call the feds."

Ethan plucked him back. "Forget the feds, they're useless. Tell me who these guys are, every detail."

"The Russians are trying to start a new diamond trade in the CAR. They've been trying to goose step the conflict diamond laws, and that's what my case is about. I represent the company that has the legitimate claim to the mines in the area, but in addition to trying to fight the war on the ground, they're trying to fight it out in court here. They're going to lose, obviously, and they're getting desperate."

"The CAR?" Ethan repeated. When he thought things couldn't get worse, they did.

"The CAR is the Central African Republic," Piedmont explained.

"I know what it is," Ethan snapped. "Is that where they took her?"

"It's where they threatened to take her," Piedmont replied. "But the feds said they couldn't get her out."

"Would you forget the feds?" Ethan said. "They're worse than useless now." He crouched and put his hands over his face, breathing deep.

"What are you doing?" Piedmont asked.

"I'm making a mental list of everything I'm going to need," Ethan said.

"What are you talking about?" Piedmont asked. "Why would you need anything? What do you have to do with this whole situation?"

"I'm the person who is going to go get her and bring her home. Shut up and let me think a minute."

"Amelia said you work for an indexing company," Piedmont said.

Ethan dropped his hands from his face to look at him with a wry smile. "Oh, so you do know who I am."

Piedmont blew out a breath. "Can you tell me what's going on without being so cryptic and condescending?"

"The CAR is a hot spot, off the charts crazy, a total no-go zone. In addition to the Russians and their diamond lust, there's Boko Haram, Isil, and local gangs who look for any opportunity to kidnap and pillage. There is no way the government will consent to sending in a team for one civilian. But they'll send a ghost, someone who can get in and out unseen. Someone who can go in and retrieve her with minimal noise and damage. That's where I come in, but I'm going to need your help."

Piedmont blinked at him, digesting the glut of surprising information. "I'll help, whatever you need. Name it."

"Give me a piece of paper," Ethan demanded. Piedmont did so, and Ethan scribbled a small list. "I need money, twenty thousand cash, and I need you to call these congressmen to clear a path. I'm going to be breaking about a hundred international laws, and I need you to get them to make it all okay. Don't get off the phone until you get them to agree, otherwise it's all going to be useless and we won't be able to get back out of Africa once I retrieve her."

Piedmont took the list and read it. "This guy lives next door. I had dinner with him last night," he noted.

Ethan rolled his eyes. "Okay, Richie Rich, get on it. Use those famous lawyer skills like you've never used them before. Amelia's life depends on it. I'm going to get the ball rolling on my end, and I'll be in contact when it's set."

They didn't say goodbye. Ethan turned and sprinted to his bike. He wanted to hop a flight right now, to singlehandedly take on the entire country, if that was what it took. But that was emotion talking. He had to be rational, to use his training and think like an agent. First thing first, he needed to confirm Amelia had actually been taken out of the country. There was only one person who could help him do that as quickly as he needed it to be done. Pulling out his phone, he searched his contacts and sent a text.

"Don't you have a hacker on your team?"

"Yes, Blue, but he's not as good as you; you're the best," Ethan said.

"Oh, Ethan, flattery will get you everywhere," Blue replied. They were at his apartment, a shockingly nice loft with a view of downtown.

"How do you afford this place?"

"I could tell you, but then I'd have to hire someone like you to kill you," Blue said. "Okay, here we go. The camera outside Amelia's apartment caught a face." Ethan leaned over his shoulder and watched grainy video of two men carrying a kicking and struggling Amelia out of her apartment and stuffing her into a trunk. One of the men turned, giving the camera enough of a glimpse to pan his face. Within seconds, Blue had his ID. "Must be an up-and-comer because we have nothing on him," Blue added. "I'm going to scan for him at airports."

"Private airports. There's no way they'd be able to smuggle her out on a commercial plane."

"Not my first go-round, young Ethan," Blue said, typing so quickly his fingers seemed in danger of flying off his hands.

"Here we go—private transport left an hour ago, and your boy was on it."

Ethan blew out a breath, fighting a wave of nausea. Amelia was out of the country, officially out of his reach. Africa was a massive continent. The flight over the ocean could go wrong in a million different ways. What if...He shook his head. "Okay, I need to know everything you can get for me about their operation in CAR, especially a location."

Blue tapped his fingers nervously on his desktop. "I'm going to have to, er, bump some satellites to redirect them. It's not exactly legal, in the legal sense of the word legal. And I'd really rather not go back to prison, much as I love little Amelia."

"Do it. I have someone paving the way with the House Intelligence Committee as we speak."

"I'm more concerned about The Colonel. The man looks at my hair and tats like he wants to personally scrape them off with broken glass," Blue said. He was a very round peg in a very square hole in the world of military intelligence.

"Ridge will handle The Colonel," Ethan said confidently.

"OK, the paper trail for their organization is easy, since they've filed court documents. I have the location, if it's legit, and now I'm moving a Russian satellite so we can get a look at the compound."

"I don't actually need you to narrate what you're doing; do it," Ethan said.

"Do you have any idea how difficult what I'm doing actually is, and how few people in the world can do it?" Blue asked.

"Absolutely, that's why I'm here," Ethan said.

"So long as we're clear on that," Blue said, appeased. He typed for a couple minutes before speaking again. "Here you go, your compound. The pictures are twenty four hours old, but unless it's blown up between now and then, it should be a current view."

Ethan stared at the grainy image. It was a shabby dwelling, a few rooms. "Print the coordinates for me. I've got to order a transport. I owe you big."

"Get in line," Blue said, turning on his printer.

An hour later, Ethan was over the ocean. Unlike Amelia, he would be flying a nonstop commercial flight into Ghana. Once there, he would take a private plane to the CAR. The plane had already been arranged, thanks to The Colonel. The man had contacts in every country, or so it seemed to anyone who knew him. But after that, Ethan would be on his own.

The flight would last ten and a half hours. Ethan forced himself to sleep, at least a few hours, but it was fitful at best. So much more could go wrong with this mission than could go right. The only thing in his favor at this point was that Amelia was being held for ransom. Piedmont Bonvoy had received the note before Ethan's departure. They had two days before the trial restarted. It would take almost that long to get to her. If Amelia hadn't called him, if Ethan hadn't gotten a jump start on things, he would never get to her in time before the ultimatum was up. Knowing the Russians, they would keep her in good shape until the date on the note. After that, they would likely kill her or sell her. She was young, blond, and beautiful and would score a tremendous price on the human trafficking circuit.

Sleep. He cleared his mind, pushing away the thoughts of everything that could go wrong. *This is what you do,* he reminded himself. *This is what you've been trained for.* He would get her out and he would bring her home, safe and unharmed, because he wouldn't allow for any other option.

With that resolution in mind, he closed his eyes and slept.

When they touched down in Ghana, his contact was waiting for him with a car that took him to another plane. The supplies had already been gathered, everything he would need while he was there, including night vision goggles, weapons, and a parachute. *Bless you, Colonel,* Ethan thought.

"You're going to jump blind in the darkness of night," the contact said. Ghana spoke English, thankfully. Ethan was a nightmare at languages.

"Wouldn't be the first time," Ethan said, though it would be the first time alone. He hadn't jumped since he was a SEAL, and then he had jumped with his team. He was more nervous than he let on.

"Watch out for the hyenas," the contact said, and Ethan didn't know if he was joking. With effort, he resisted the urge to pull out his phone and Google whether or not hyenas ate people. Like most carnivores, they were probably looking for an easy target. He wouldn't be one, unless he landed wrong and broke a leg and then, well, he'd face that catastrophe if it happened.

In seemingly no time, they were in the air and flying again for another four hours. Unlike the commercial flight, this one was choppy and nausea inducing. Ethan fought against it by eating power bars and downing water. He needed to stay fed and hydrated for the mission. After the jump, he would have to sprint three miles to town and then do whatever needed to be done once he reached the compound. Eating and drinking were necessary, despite how much his body rebelled.

"Circling the jump zone," the pilot said, his pleasant accent ringing in Ethan's headset. "Jump at your discretion. Weather's clear; you have a fifteen minute window."

Ethan stood and removed the headset and oxygen mask and then opened the heavy metal door, a task in and of itself. After a few deep breaths that didn't feel deep because of the altitude, he opened his eyes and plunged into the inky blackness below, free falling for ninety seconds before he pulled the cord. On a normal day, it would have been fun. He loved to skydive. It had been one of his favorite parts of being in the navy. And even in the midst of his stress, the free fall worked to clear his mind, to ease his anxiety. While he was falling, cushioned only by air, he felt as if everything would be all right.

It was a perfect jump and an even better landing. No broken bones, no drag marks. He landed on his feet and removed the chute, tossing it aside. Someone would find it in the daylight and wonder what it had all been about, and then they would likely sell it for whatever cash it could bring.

He tightened the backpack and checked his compass, finding northeast, and then he ran, a flat out sprint that landed him three miles in eighteen minutes. *What happened to the five-minute miles of my youth?*

He wondered as he bent double, sucking oxygen. When he could rightfully breathe again, he straightened, opened his pack, and put on his gear—Kevlar, helmet, goggles, guns and knives. When he was ready, he attached his watch, the one that had been programed with the compound's GPS coordinates. It was a little over a mile away, and he wouldn't run this time. Not only would it use precious energy, but his gear was too heavy and there was too much risk of being seen. As soon as his feet touched dirt in the Central African Republic, he ceased to exist. If he died while he was on this assignment, his parents would be told he'd been killed in a car accident. If he was caught, the official response would be, "Oops, sorry, we didn't know. Do with him what you will." As far as the US government was concerned, he was completely on his own, a lone wolf gone rogue, at least officially. Unofficially, they were bending the waters to ease his trip, doing everything they could to try and bring him and Amelia home safe again.

As he journeyed to his destination, he slid behind buildings, slipped between alleys, sidled by houses. For all intents and purposes, he was a ghost, helped along by the fact that the area in question lacked electricity almost completely.

When he reached the compound, he withdrew the thermal imager from his pack and held it aloft. There were five bodies inside. Two large ones in the front, two large ones in the back and one smaller, prone one in the middle. He hoped Amelia was merely sleeping and could be roused. If she were unconscious, he would have to carry her out, impeding their escape. He lowered the scanner and thought, trying to conjure a plan. On missions, Ridge had been the planner. Ethan was the go-ahead guy, the point man willing to insert himself gleefully into any situation, no matter how dangerous. Since becoming an agent, he'd had more practice at the thinking side of things, but it wasn't his strong suit.

Should he take out all four guards and then retrieve her or take out two, get her, and then take the other two? If he tried to take out all four, one or more might have the chance to get to Amelia first, to use her as a shield or leverage. But if he took out two and then got her, he would have to take them out while she was with him, thereby scarring her for life.

The safest option was to take them two by two. If Amelia thought less of him after watching him work, he would deal with that later. For now, her safety was the priority.

The silencer was already on his gun. He slipped in the back of the compound and dropped the two guards without a sound, pausing only to check for a pulse once they were disabled. He didn't want any nasty surprises springing up behind him once his back was turned. There wouldn't be with these two, however; they were gone.

Silently, he slid down the hallway and opened the door to Amelia's room. She was lying in the middle of the darkened room, curled in a ball. Her back was to him, and she was trembling. She hadn't yet detected his presence. He eased forward and pressed his palm to her mouth. She twisted, kicking and fighting to get away from him. He pinned her and spoke in her ear.

"It's me."

She went so still so suddenly that he was afraid she'd passed out. *"Ethan?"* she mouthed. He nodded and remembered she couldn't see him. In the blackness of her room, he was the only one wearing night vision goggles.

"Yes. I'm going to get you out of here. Don't make a sound, follow my lead. There are two guards at the front." He paused. "When we reach them, close your eyes. Don't watch. Don't listen."

She nodded. He reached for her hands and found them bound with rope. He removed his knife and cut through the thick ropes like butter. Her feet were similarly bound, and he also made short work of those ropes. He started to pull her up, but she held back, shaking out her hands.

"Numb," she mouthed.

Ethan ground his teeth. She had probably been bound the entire time, which, by his calculation, was more than twenty four hours. She winced as he rubbed her ankles and wrists, trying to force the blood back into them. After a minute she sat up and then, leaning on him, tentatively rose off the bed and took a tottering step. Her leg collapsed and he caught her, helping her take a few more steps until the circulation returned completely and she was able to stand and walk on her own. Ethan's heart thundered with anxiety. Any minute the guards would discover their fallen partners and come for them. They would be boxed in this room like cows before slaughter.

He didn't want to rush her, but he had to. "We have to go. Now."

She nodded and straightened, trying not to wince as she fell into line behind him and followed him from the room. She was trying so hard to be brave and strong when he knew what she most wanted to do was fall apart and weep while he held her. *Later,* he wanted to say. There would be time for tears and comfort later.

When they reached the guards, he gave her a light shove away from him and took them out. The first one didn't see him coming, but the second one did, alerted by the thud of his partner's body. He leapt for Ethan. They struggled a bit, but it was over quickly. He turned to retrieve Amelia and saw her eyes squeezed together, her hands over her ears, behaving exactly as he'd told her. Blocking her view as much as possible, he gathered her wrists and spoke.

"It's over. Keep your eyes up as we go by, don't look down. Promise me."

"I promise," she whispered, her voice croaky with sleep and disuse. She had likely never seen a dead body before; he wanted to keep it that way.

They made their way around the guards and outside to one of the Jeeps. Ethan hotwired the car and they took off toward the west, toward the embassy in Cameroon and safety.

CHAPTER 13

Conversation was impossible. What passed for roads in the country was nothing more than a glorified collection of mud and potholes. The Jeep lacked both shocks and power steering and bounced them around violently. Occasionally they saw people out and about, but Ethan didn't stop, not until the Jeep sputtered and died, out of gas, did he bail and lift Amelia down.

"Where are we?" she asked.

"We're in a country in the dead center of Africa, the Central African Republic."

"But the people who took me are Russian," Amelia said.

"There's a big Russian presence in Africa. Long story short, you're caught up in a war over conflict diamonds, blood diamonds."

"Piedmont's trying a case over diamonds," she said.

"I know," he said, teeth gritted.

"Oh," she drawled, making the connection.

"Amelia, are you hurt? Did they hurt you?" He cupped her face in his hand, searching her eyes.

She shook her head.

"The truth. You can tell me anything, you know that."

"They drugged me to knock me out when we reached the airport, and they tossed me around a bit. But other than that, they didn't touch me." She paused. "They didn't rape me, if that's what you're asking."

He hugged her, pressing her tight against his chest. "You're going to be okay."

"I *am* okay," she assured him. "It was scary, but it's over now."

"Um, not quite," he said. He let her go so he could see her face. "This country, the CAR, it's not doing so well right now. In fact, it's really, really, really dangerous, and you should know I've been a lot of dangerous places and therefore don't say that lightly. Assume everyone we see here wants to kill, kidnap, or rob us, not necessarily in that order. I'm not sure which of us is a higher priority target—you because you're blond and pretty or me because I'm an American agent."

She smiled. "Hey, you admitted it."

"After this, I don't think we're going to have any secrets between us," Ethan said.

She rested her hands on his biceps. "Ethan, I will do whatever you need me to do, I can help however you want. Tell me what to do, and I'll do it. We're going to get out of this, I can feel it."

"The optimistic good cheer is a step in the right direction. First we need to get gas, and then we need to find a place to stay. We also have to find a robe and scarf for you to try and tone down the pretty. You're like a flashing neon sign that says, 'Kidnap and sell me, please.'"

"That might have been more graphic information than I actually needed, but alrighty then. Let's get gas, find lodging, and cover me up. Do you think maybe we could work food into that equation?"

"Did they feed you at all or give you any water?" he asked.

She shook her head.

"Aw, baby, I'm sorry. I didn't even think. Here." He rifled in his pack and handed her a power bar and bottle of water. "Don't drink any tap water. Don't even brush your teeth with it." He was slightly worried about her health. He had been inoculated against everything, up to and including anthrax. She'd had none of the requisite shots one needed when venturing to Africa. She was susceptible to everything, adding another layer of danger to an already dangerous scenario. "Don't touch any animals, and especially not dogs or cats."

"Why?"

"Rabies."

"Rabies is actually a thing here?" she asked.

"Everything is a thing here. Are you current on any vaccinations?"

She nodded. "The salon made me get boosters for nearly everything, Hep-A, Hep-B, MMR, a T-Dap and the flu shot."

"Good, that's good. Just do what I said, try not to touch anything, wash your hands as much as possible, and tell me if you get bitten by a mosquito."

"Is there anything in Africa that doesn't want to kill me?" she asked.

He picked her up and brought her level with his face. "Me." He kissed her cheek and set her down again.

"A cheek kiss, really? You just saved my life like flipping Jason Bourne, we're five thousand miles from home, may never get back again, and you kissed my cheek?" she said. "That's not what the hero's supposed to do. Have you never watched a movie or read a book?"

"I need to focus on my mission. After that, we'll talk," he said.

"Talk. Can't wait. Maybe things will get crazy and we'll end up *conversing*." She faked a gasp and covered her mouth.

"After this, we'll 'talk,'" he said, using air quotes. "Better?"

"You're on the right track," she said.

Ethan had no idea how it was possible to be having fun in their current situation, but he was. He took her hand and headed toward the makeshift little town on the horizon, hoping it hadn't been overrun by terrorists or Russians or gangsters, hoping to find one good person to help them out. Mostly he was hoping to find one person who spoke English and not French, the national language.

When they arrived, he saw no signs of Boko Haram or Isil, but he also found no one who spoke anything but French. He must have said *Parlez vous Anglais* fifteen times before Amelia rolled her eyes and busted out an entire paragraph in flowing French.

Someone answered her in kind. She nodded a few times and spoke back to him. Ethan stood looking between them like the hapless moron he was.

"He has gas. He'll sell it to us for a hundred dollars, American," she said at last.

"What just happened here?" he asked, slack jawed and dumbfounded.

Amelia bit her finger, feigning innocence. "Did I not mention French was my minor? My family thought it was, in my brother's words, the stupidest, most frivolous minor on the planet. Who's laughing now, Darren?"

"I am," Ethan said, chuckling. "Are you ever going to stop surprising me?"

"No," she said.

"Good. Tell him to get the gas, and I'll give him the money. Also see if he can get some sort of cover for you." She turned to the man, said more words, motioned to her body and hair, and he disappeared. "Knowing you're fluent in French might have been handy information, chicklet." He poked her waist.

"It's the middle of Africa. How was I to know they spoke French here? I thought it would be Swahili."

"This used to be a French colony, and so was Cameroon," he said, feeling much more cheerful over their prospects. The language barrier had been one of his biggest concerns, and now that was gone.

The man returned with the gas and a robe and scarf for Amelia, and they paid him the money. "Ask him if he knows a good, safe place to stay the night, west." He pointed to the west. Amelia asked him the question and relayed the answer.

"He said to get off the main road before you hit the border. The gangs keep a lookout for cars and trucks and there are often raiders. Going by foot is a safer bet. He said anywhere the terrorists haven't invaded would be a good idea for lodging."

They thanked the man. Amelia donned the robe and green flowered headscarf that, in true Amelia fashion, was quite becoming. "You're not supposed to look even better in that getup," Ethan groused.

"I'm sorry, but headscarves are kind of in right now. I wear them a lot, actually. This one's super cute. I wonder where I could get some more."

"I can't believe we're trying to escape this country with our lives and you're contemplating where to shop," he said.

"You don't hear me complaining and trying to get you to stop being a commando, do you? You be you, and I'll be me," she said, frowning.

"That wasn't a complaint, it was more of an observation. I like you exactly as you are, you know that."

"Better than your dry cleaner?" she asked.

"I don't know, Mr. Kim is pretty sweet," he said. He reached for her hand and gave it a squeeze. "I already told you I was sorry."

"I know, but you hurt my feelings."

"I was trying to; I wanted to push you away," he said.

"Why?" she asked.

He shrugged. "To see if you'd come back. It's a thing I do, but I'm working on it. I'm trying not to with you."

"Ethan," she said.

"Hmm," he replied.

"I'm still here," she said, giving his hand a hard squeeze.

"Hey, Amelia."

"Yes?"

"I'm still here, too. And I'm usually long gone by now."

"I know," she said. He liked that she didn't ask anything of him, didn't broach the future, didn't press him for more. She just smiled and gave him the look, the tender one that said she thought he was worthy, a man to be admired.

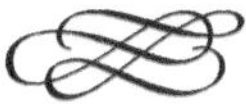

CHAPTER 14

They made it a few hundred more miles until the gas gave out again. By that time they were close enough to the border to give up on the Jeep entirely and go by foot.

Ethan could have made it across the border, but Amelia was exhausted. She'd been through an ordeal, physically and emotionally traumatized, and she'd had one power bar in the last thirty-six hours. And yet she didn't complain.

"I think you could have made it as a SEAL," he told her, putting his arm around her shoulders and drawing her close so he could kiss her temple.

"I'm not the strongest swimmer," she said. "But if I understand the SEALs correctly, it's not necessary to be good in the water."

"Spot on. There was very little water training involved, as long as you don't count pretty much everything we did."

"I knew I was right," she said, squeezing his waist. "Is Africa where you go when you pretend to go to Canada?"

"Yes, but not here. This area's too far gone. I usually go to Nigeria, Libya, Morocco, Egypt. Sometimes Liberia and Somalia."

"Are you going to have to kill me now that you've told me the truth about your life?" she asked.

"No, but I might have to do something else with you," he said. His hand smoothed up and down her arm. "Cold?"

"Yes, that's precisely why I have goose bumps. Brr." She feigned chafing her hands up and down her arms.

Ethan laughed and then stopped short, studying the town before them.

"What's the problem?" Amelia whispered.

"That woman was wearing a burka," he said.

"So am I," she said.

He shook his head. "You're wearing robes and a scarf."

"What's the difference?"

"About twenty pounds of fabric. Think of the difference in our country between someone who is a conservative evangelical and someone who is old-order Amish."

"Why is it concerning she's wearing a burka?" Amelia asked.

"It means the area's been infested by either Boko Haram or Isil," he said. "It means this area is hostile and dangerous."

"Can't we go around?" she asked.

He shook his head. "Stay behind me, keep your head down, don't speak unless I tell you to, and do exactly what I say."

"Okay," she agreed, taking a step behind him and dropping her eyes demurely.

If the area had been infested, the only chance they had of making it through was making people believe they weren't alone. "Amelia, if I lie, don't show it. Don't act surprised. Go along with it, no matter what I say. Got it?"

She nodded.

"Okay, here we go." He took her hand and they walked the remaining mile to town.

Amelia felt conspicuous, as if everyone was staring at her. She wasn't sure if all of Ethan's warnings had made her paranoid or if it was because people were actually staring at her. She had rarely been more afraid, mostly because she knew Ethan was afraid. He was one of the most fearless, adventure-loving people she had ever met. If something made him nervous, it was because there was good reason to be nervous.

They made it a half-mile or so when a man holding a gun stepped out of a building and yelled for them to stop. Ethan kept going, and it occurred to Amelia that he had no idea what the man said.

"He told us to stop," she whispered.

Ethan stopped and faced the man, tucking Amelia behind him.

"Who are you and why are you here?" the man demanded. Amelia translated. Ethan answered, and she translated that, too.

"My team and I are mercenaries sent by an animal rights group to stop the rhino poachers. We became separated on a raid. This is my translator. They're waiting over the border."

The man regarded them, looking them up and down. Amelia tried to look brave and important, a nearly impossible task when she was close to losing bladder control.

"How many of you are there?" the man asked.

"Twenty," Ethan replied without missing a beat.

"All American?"

Ethan shook his head. "Mostly Australian, some New Zealand. Besides myself there are three other Americans. If we don't meet when we're supposed to, they'll come to find us." He was holding his weapon, Amelia realized. It was tucked against his chest, but it was in plain view and his hand was on the trigger. He might actually shoot this man. The man might shoot them. They were a hairsbreadth away from being a free-for-all, based on the believability of Ethan's lie.

He looked Amelia up and down and spoke to Ethan. "Is the translator for sale?"

Ethan shook his head, his hand tightening on the gun. "We're leaving now, getting out of the country before the poachers retaliate."

The man frowned, looking to the east. "The poachers are coming here?"

"They're a couple of hours behind us, armed and angry."

The man was now frowning at the eastern horizon, his hand tightening on his gun. "Go," he directed, nodding his head in the opposite direction.

Ethan didn't need to be told twice. He turned and walked briskly away, practically dragging Amelia behind him. When they were safely out of town, she spoke.

"Can you explain to me why that worked?"

"American agents are high-value targets, but no one cares about mercenaries. They like Australians better than they like Americans who have the stigma of being Americans attached wherever we go. And 'the enemy of my enemy is my friend' came into play. They don't like the poachers, a brutal, ruthless group, and the poachers don't like them, a brutal, ruthless group. Pitting them against each other was enough to buy us an escape."

"What will happen when the poachers don't show up?" she asked.

"Nothing. Maybe he'll figure out I was lying or maybe he'll think the poachers heard they were arming up and changed their minds. Either way, he won't pursue us."

"How do you know?"

"Because he was emaciated and barefoot. He doesn't have the energy for wild goose chases against an armed man. Like all predators, he was looking for an easy target. We weren't one."

"That's brilliant," Amelia said.

"Thank you, but this is kind of what I do for a living," he said. They walked in silence a while before she spoke again.

"Ethan, please don't resent what I'm about to say, but how can you consider quitting to become a high school football coach? I mean, don't get me wrong, shaping young minds is important. But you could do that on a volunteer basis. A lot of men could coach football, but only one in a few hundred thousand could do what you do, and you're so, so incredibly good at it."

"It's different when you're here," he said.

"How so? Do you bumble like the Nutty Professor when I'm not with you? Drop your gun and accidently shoot yourself in the foot? Yell out classified information whenever you get nervous?" she asked. Somehow she couldn't imagine him being bad at anything.

"No, but having you with me gives me a purpose. Keeping you safe and well is my number one priority. I have a clear objective. I always had a clear objective in the SEALs. Most of the time at work, I don't. I follow bad guys around and take pictures, tail important men to make sure they haven't gone rogue. It feels boring and pointless."

"Can't you transfer somewhere else? I mean, Maggie and Ridge seem to do a lot of stuff that has a point, a clear objective. Why can't you work with them?"

He opened his mouth and closed it again. "To be honest with you, I never considered it. This is where The Colonel placed me, so this is where I've been. I'm used to taking orders from people who rank higher. But you're right, there's no reason I have to stay here when I hate it so much. I'm not in the navy anymore. I can switch jobs, I can go where I want, do what I want."

"You're a real boy, Pinocchio," she agreed.

Laughing, he picked her up and twirled her around. "This little talk has been life changing. You have no idea."

"It was almost worth getting kidnapped and taken to Africa by armed Russians so we could have this moment," she said.

He laughed again and set her down. "You are a crazy child. This is not a laughable situation, especially because we're about to enter Carnot."

"What's bad about that?"

"A few years ago it erupted into crazy violence."

"Boko Haram or Isil?" she guessed.

"Neither, an anti-Muslim group, a local tribe. They rounded people up, killed them with machetes, forced them out of the city. It's better, but crazy volatile. It could erupt again at literally any moment. We can't stay here. Our number one objective is to score a ride to Gamboula, a border city."

"Why can't we go all the way to Cameroon tonight?" she asked.

"Because you don't have a passport. We're going to have to sneak in," he said.

"Oh, is that all?" she asked. "We just have to survive a night in a country that wants to kill us so we can sneak into another country that wants to do the same?"

"Once we get out of the northern part of Cameroon, it will be better, as long as we don't go too far west because they're fighting in that part, too. Southern Cameroon is on the ocean. It's kind a resort place, believe it or not."

"Will we have time to go to a spa?" she asked.

"You've got to be joking," he said.

"I am," she assured him.

"Good because I promised your boyfriend I would return you safe and sound as soon as possible. And Maggie and Ridge, I have no idea if they know we're gone. I couldn't get ahold of them before I left. The Colonel was going to try."

"Quick question: who is The Colonel? Because every time you mention him, I picture the unseen villain in *Inspector Gadget*, the one who sits in the chair and pets the cat."

"That's probably a fair depiction. The Colonel is my boss. Actually, my boss's boss. He's the intermediary between us and Congress."

"Do you like him?" she asked.

"If by 'like' you mean fear and respect? Then yes, I like him so much I tremble every time he enters the room."

"Am I allowed to talk in this town?" she asked.

"I think so," he said. "Was there something particular you wanted to say?"

"Yes. 'Where is food'?" she said.

Carnot was a bigger city. They followed the sounds to an outdoor market where people had laid their wares in the dirt. Amelia stopped to look at several stalls and, despite his scoffing, bought a headscarf. Several street vendors were selling food. They bought the cleanest looking, best smelling morsels along with bottles of Coke. The Coke was warm, but so was the food, and Amelia thought it delicious. The bread reminded her of naan, only thinner, and she also ate okra and some type of meat.

"Goat, if I had to guess," Ethan said. When their bellies were full, they found someone to give them a ride to Gamboula. He saw Ethan's gun and nodded in approval, adding his own weaponry into the mix.

"The road is danger," he said when he saw Amelia eyeing his gun. It was something they'd already been warned about.

Despite the danger, despite the painful bouncing on the rutted road, it was nice to rest a while, to sit in the back seat with Ethan and feel his arms around her, safe, warm, and secure. If not for the fact that she had to hold on tightly to avoid being bounced out of the car, she might have fallen asleep.

The driver took them to a place he knew in Gamboula, a makeshift hotel of sorts that would keep them overnight. It was basically a tiny room in someone's home, but it was private, and they had indoor plumbing. After taking turns in the bathroom, they met back in the bedroom, eyeing the tiny bed. Amelia peeled off the hot, heavy robe until she was wearing only her shorts and t-shirt, unwound her hair, and climbed in, patting the spot beside her.

Ethan set his pack on the floor beside the bed and climbed in beside her, still wearing his Kevlar vest.

"That vest may be bullet-proof, but it won't protect you from my advances," she said.

"I'm sorry, but years of training have taught me I need to be ready to roll at a moment's notice in situations like these," he said.

"When an attractive woman is beside you making kissy faces?" she asked, scrunching her lips together in an exaggerated kiss.

"When a town could be thrown over by an armed militia at any moment and we might have to flee for our lives," he clarified.

"Oh, that," she said. She rested her palm on his chest. "I can't even feel your heart through that thing."

"That's how you know it's well made," he said. "They tried making thin, see-through ones that had a big outline of the heart on them, but they weren't popular sellers among soldiers and policemen for some reason."

"I'm glad you're protected, but I was really hoping for a bit of warm comfort tonight," she admitted, sounding uncharacteristically serious and maybe a little bit needy. Her cheerful demeanor had fooled him into forgetting how much she'd been through the last couple of days and how much it had to be affecting her.

He sat up, took off the vest, laid it on his pack, lay back down, and opened his arms to her. She snuggled close to him, resting her head on his heart. His hand smoothed over her hair.

"Thank you," she murmured.

"You're right, this is way better," he said.

"I meant thank you for everything. Thank you for coming to get me, for saving my life."

"Don't mention it." His hand continued a slow progression over her head. "I mean really don't mention it. You could get me fired or prosecuted."

"Your job's a secret, I get it," she said, slightly annoyed.

"Not from you, not anymore. I've needed someone to talk to about things, but I couldn't because of clearance. But I don't think you count as one of the people I'm not allowed to talk to anymore."

"I'm glad to hear that," she said, her fingers trailing lightly over his chest. "Hey, Ethan Becket, Becket Ethan."

"Mm," he said. He was getting drowsy. The room was warm and the gentle pressure of Amelia's head on his chest was immensely comforting.

"I'm in love with you."

His eyes popped open; he was wide-awake now. "Oh. I…"

She shifted slightly and pressed her fingers to his lips. "I don't want a response, that's not why I said it. I said it because I thought I was going to die, and when that happens, life takes on unusual clarity. Priorities shift, and fear falls away. I'm telling you because I think you should know, regardless of how you feel or where you stand." She rested her head on his chest again. "I didn't want it to be you. I tried so hard to make it Piedmont. Piedmont is a good man. He's handsome, funny, smart, sweet, attentive, and so wonderfully, beautifully rich. You should see his house. I mean, I could cry thinking about it. He's twenty-eight, and he has an actual art collection. You're twenty-eight, and you have a toaster. Your apartment is as crummy as mine, prob-ably crummier because a lot of times it smells like unwashed gym socks. He's been talking marriage and children. You lack the emotional capacity to even send me one of those 'do you like me, circle one yes or no' notes. But Piedmont has this one glaring char-acter flaw: he's not you."

He resumed sifting his fingers through her hair and, after a few minutes of silence, she was asleep. Ethan, meanwhile, lay awake for a long, long time.

CHAPTER 15

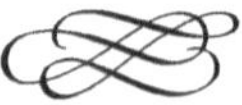

In the morning when Amelia woke, Ethan was gone. "Ethan?" she called, but there was no answer. She got up to check the bathroom, just in case. When she returned to the bedroom, she saw a note on his pillow.

"Went to find a scout. Don't panic, be back soon. STAY THERE! EB."

With time to kill, she decided to take a shower. She tracked down their hosts and asked for soap. They gave her a bar of good-smelling soap in fancy French wrapping. Amelia washed and then washed again, not caring the water ran cold the entire time. She didn't have a toothbrush or paste, and Ethan had said not to use the water to brush her teeth anyway, so she settled for gargling mouthwash. She was finger combing her hair when Ethan returned, and right away she knew things were awkward between them.

"Hey, you showered," he said.

"Nothing gets by you highly trained spies," she said.

"Yeah, heh," he said with a lame chuckle. "So, I found a scout and he's going to take us across. It'll be a water crossing in his boat."

"Okay." Was she supposed to protest? He was looking at her like she might.

"If I shower, am I going to smell like you?" he asked after a few beats of painful silence.

"If we're lucky," she said.

He grinned and she gripped the edge of the bed to keep from flinging herself into his arms. "I remember a certain young lady telling me once that she liked my sweat smell."

"She sounds weird. You should avoid anyone who speaks favorably about BO."

"I can't seem to get away from her. I go to sleep, she's there. I wake up, she's there. I fall asleep, she's in my dreams."

"Try going to another country. I bet she can't find you there," Amelia said.

"You'd think so, but she's clever," he said. "Some kind of French-speaking math genius."

"Nerd alert," Amelia replied.

The heavy silence returned and lingered. She got the sense he wanted to say something, that he was trying to tell her something, but she didn't want to hear it. "You should take that shower now."

He nodded and backed out of the room, keeping his eyes on her until he was out of range. When he was gone, Amelia flopped backwards onto the bed. Why had she told him she loved him? She'd clearly scared him away, possibly forever. She had never pursued a man, never made the first move. Men had always pursued her, and that was how she liked it. She'd had a serious high school boyfriend for two solid years and never once told him she loved him. Why did she have to start being forward and desperate with Ethan? Had a kidnapping and near-death experience knocked her so far off-kilter? Well, that would do it if anything would. Maybe he would understand. Maybe he wouldn't think less of her for basically throwing herself at him emotionally.

"Watcha doing?" Suddenly Ethan was leaning over her, one hand pressed to the mattress on either side of her head.

"Bah!" she yelped, jumping. "Do you have to be so sneaky?"

"Kind of, yeah. In fact, it's literally in my work contract," he said.

She could feel her cheeks heating with the memory of last night's confession. He must think she was some kind of stupid kid who couldn't keep a cap on her feelings. She *knew* he couldn't give her more than he already was, and yet she had pushed him by making her grand confession.

He eased in closer. "Tell me, and be honest. Do I smell better?" His lips were *right there*, so close all she had to do was tilt her head and claim them. What was he doing to her? Was he toying with her? Had last night's confession made him cocky?

"You'll do," she all but gasped. His lips brushed hers, but before she could claim them, he moved on, easing them out of range.

"Amelia," he whispered. His teeth scraped her jaw.

"Mm," she said, closing her eyes. She was holding on to her self-control with a feather grip.

"I need to tell you something." His left hand slid to her hip, pulling her closer.

"Go on," she urged. *Please, please go on.* Was she allowed to touch him in this scenario? It had been so long ago that she kissed him in Maggie's pantry, and yet she remembered the feel of those kisses as if it was only yesterday. Ethan kissed as well as he did everything else, and he had opened a chasm within her that night, a deep well that could only be filled by him and his touch. Piedmont had had no effect on the yawning space within her, the one reserved for Ethan. And now it was about to happen again. Finally, she would be released from months of agonized misery and longing.

"I had a date, the night you got taken, and...."

She scrambled away from him and propped herself at the head of the bed. A date? He'd had a date with another woman, and he was telling her about it in the middle of making a move on her. He must be feeling guilty for cheating on his new love interest, the same way Amelia was feeling guilty over Piedmont. "Oh. All right. Well, you're a free agent. I mean, technically I have a boyfriend. I should probably call him. Can I call him from here?"

He moved back, scowling. "No, you cannot call him from here. This isn't a 7-11. There's no payphone."

"Don't we need to go?" she said. "The border crossing and all that?"

With a sigh, he stood upright and took a step away from her. "Yes, let's go."

Their host had provided breakfast for them, more okra with some kind of beans. Ethan paid the man, and they were on their way.

"I must be the most expensive date ever," she said. She was blathering, but she couldn't seem to help herself. "I mean, not that this is a date, but you've spent so much. I can pay you back. Not me, exactly because, after moving and laying out a deposit in DC, my last bank statement said, 'Have you considered playing the lottery?' But I'm sure my parents would be willing…"

"It's not my money," he snapped, cutting her off. "It belongs to your boyfriend."

"Oh. Awkward."

"I'm sure you'll be earning it back after the wedding, when you combine assets. Your crummy apartment and nonexistent savings account plus his townhome, art collection, and ridiculously fluffy robes. When I grabbed him and threw him against the wall, it was like I was manhandling Bugs Bunny. You know I asked him for twenty thousand dollars to come get you, and he didn't even bat a lash. He didn't have to go to the bank, either. I think maybe he pulled it out from loose bills that had fallen between the seats. I could be a criminal, for all he knows. I could have been lying or extorting him, but he didn't seem to mind. He handed over a wad of cash and that was that. He must really love you." He darted a glance at her. She remained staring stoically ahead.

"Or maybe he felt guilty. I mean, it is kind of his fault you're here. He got a threatening letter and everything."

"Stop it," she said.

"What? I'm stating facts here. Fact: your guy is loaded. Fact: he seems to love you a lot. Fact: he received a letter threatening to kidnap you and kept it a secret so as not to violate your delicate sensibilities. Fact: he seemed A-Okay with letting another man do the dirty work of coming to get you."

"Fact: you told me you're seeing someone while your lips were very much on my jaw."

"Fact: those were my teeth."

"Fact: shut up."

"Fact: your cheeks turn pink when you're jealous," he said. She opened her mouth to reply, but he preempted her. "Final fact, we're here." They stopped beside a swollen, dirty river. A man was there with a tiny, dinged up boat.

"Are there crocodiles in this river?" she asked the man in French.

"*Oui.*"

She shuddered.

"What did you ask him?" Ethan asked.

"If he thought you were too arrogant and I could do better," she said. He snickered, causing the scout to tilt his head at him in confusion. Amelia swallowed down her anxiety and her irritation and allowed Ethan to take a hand and help her into the boat. It rocked unsteadily back and forth and she gripped the sides.

Ethan leaned forward to whisper in her ear. "I would never let you drown. You know that, right?"

"Would you let me be eaten by crocodiles?" she asked, naming her other pending fear.

"And let them mess up your Brazilian blowout? Not a chance. I had to look up what that was, by the way. Not nearly as exciting or erotic as it sounded. Does it really cost five hundred dollars?"

"Only when I do it, not when I receive it," she said. "There's such a thing as an employee discount."

"We have that, too. Buy two boxes of armor-piercing ammo, get a silencer free."

He was making her laugh, and she kind of hated him for it. How did he run so hot and cold all the time so she was forever off-balance with him?

"Amelia, don't be mad at me," he pled. "You're all I've got here."

"We'll be home soon enough," she replied.

He leaned in closer, tipping her face to his. "You're all I've got in this world."

"Don't say things like that."

"You think I'm exaggerating? You have a big, loving family. I have you and a few SEAL guys. If I died over here, they would put a tiny paragraph in my hometown paper in Vermont, and that would be that."

"How can you say things like that when you're so incredibly vital? The work you do..." she trailed off, motioning helplessly around them. "Who else can do it?"

"What's the point of saving the world if you don't have anyone to save it for?" he asked.

"I don't understand you, Becket. You push me away, you hold me close, you tease me until I want to scream, and then you say things that make me want to cry. Sometimes I really want to punch you in the nose, and other times I want to..."

"Do go on," he prompted. He took her hand and caressed it gently between both of his.

"But all the time, I want to know what's going on inside your head, inside your heart, and you won't tell me," she said.

"How can you not know?" he asked.

"Not know what?" she asked, and the boat bumped dry land, knocking them askew so that Ethan was forced to put out a hand to keep her from tumbling into the river.

"We're here," the scout announced unnecessarily, and also in English. "You two put on a good show. Most entertaining. And, *oui*, I do think he is too arrogant and you too good for him."

"Thank you, Mr. Boatman," Amelia said, waving cheerfully as they disembarked.

"Ready?" Ethan asked, taking her hand.

"For what?" she asked.

"Anything is possible," he said, and then the shot rang out.

CHAPTER 16

"*Arrêtez!*" A man in uniform was shouting at them in French to stop. He had fired his gun into the air to get their attention.

"Now is when we run," Ethan said, grabbing Amelia's hand and dragging her behind him. With her free hand, she held up her robe. She was in good shape and worked out most days, but she had nothing on him. They darted into a large grove of nearby trees and hid.

"Calm your breathing," he whispered. "Be silent. Don't move."

She wasn't sure why she needed to be quiet. Their presence had disturbed the monkeys and birds that were now shrieking all around them. If the guard could hear her breathing over all of that, he must be bionic. But she did as she was told, trying hard to calm her racing heart and erratic breathing. When he was certain the guard had given up on them, Ethan sat up and rested his head on the tree behind them.

"We're going to have to go at night," he whispered. "I had no idea they patrolled this patch so diligently."

"What would happen if they caught us?" she asked.

"Hard to say. Best case scenario, we get arrested. Worst case scenario, we get killed or kidnapped and…

"Sold into slavery," she finished the sentence for him. "Is there any scenario on this entire continent where that's not your imagined worst possible ending for me?"

"There is one more that keeps me up at night. I do all the hard work of getting you safely to the embassy, and then your boyfriend shows up with a ring and sweeps you off to a wedding."

"Piedmont doesn't like the idea of flying over the ocean," she said.

"Why? In first class they'll give him another fluffy robe," he said.

"You have to let the robe thing go."

"I've never worn a robe in my life. There are robe men, and then there are not. I am not," he said.

"You barely wear pants, Becket. If it were up to you, you'd wear boxers everywhere."

"No, I very much wouldn't. I would be al fresco, as God intended."

She groaned and put her hands over her ears. "That's way, way too much information for our level of friendship."

"You'd better get used to it because eventually these clothes are going to come off in your presence, and you'll be lucky if I ever put them back on again," he warned.

"Don't let my mother hear you talk like that. She has explicit ideas about how ladies and gentlemen should talk, especially in mixed company."

"When am I going to meet your mother?" he asked.

"Didn't you meet her at the wedding?"

"Yes, but that was in my capacity as Ridge's groomsman. I need to re-meet her in my capacity as your special friend, wink, wink."

"You don't say wink, wink."

"I just did," he said.

"No, I mean you're supposed to wink, wink."

"That's what I did. Amelia, look." He pointed to his eye and winked. "Wink, wink."

"Ethan, look." She pointed to her eye and winked twice. "See, the words aren't necessary. You don't have to narrate everything your body does. No one says 'breathe, breathe,' or 'swallow, swallow,' or 'walk, walk.'"

"What else can you teach me about life, smart girl?" he asked, leaning against the tree and smiling at her.

"So many things. I don't know where to begin," she said.

"You might as well start now. This is going to be a long day of waiting," he noted.

"I'm guessing you've had more than your share of those," she said. When he nodded, she continued. "What did you guys do to pass the time, back in the day?"

"We talked."

"About what?"

"Women mostly," he said. "But also other random things. We shared stories, opened up, spilled our guts."

"Let's do that," she said.

"You can't plan to do it. It happens naturally."

"That's because you're a man."

"Thank you for noticing; I've been working hard at it," he said.

"What I meant was that women don't have to naturally evolve into friendships. We sit down and talk about things on purpose. Let me show you how it's done: What was your first job?"

"Lifeguard at the local pool."

She rolled her eyes.

"What?" he asked.

"I'm picturing the hordes of teenage girls who tried to drown in your presence on a daily basis," she said.

"There were a lot, and there was one legit almost drowning. He was a two-year-old little boy whose mom became distracted by another kid. All of a sudden I looked over and this boy was standing in water over his head, arms up, not thrashing, not moving, just standing there. And that's what drowning looks like. So I jumped in, pulled him out, and gave him mouth to mouth while someone called an ambulance. He coughed up an ocean of water, but he was fine."

"That's amazing," she said.

"It was my first taste of saving someone, and I was kind of hooked after that. I knew I wanted to do something in public service, something to help others."

"Do you ever wonder if someday in heaven you'll see all the people you've saved?" she asked.

"I spend more time worrying I'll be somewhere else with all the people I've killed," he admitted.

She petted his head, frowning.

"Hey, I just realized something. Last week Ridge said you're twenty three. How is it possible you're another year older?"

"I don't know, but it keeps happening every year. I'm beginning to think it's some sort of code or pattern," she said.

"I missed your birthday, huh?"

She nodded.

"Ugh, I'm so sorry. I'm really bad with stuff like that. I feel terrible."

"It's fine. My therapist and I had a productive discussion for several hours about it, and I feel in time I'll be able to move on," she said, smiling.

"No, it's bad. You made my birthday so fun, and I didn't even talk to you on yours," he said.

"Um, yes, you did," she said.

He covered his face. "I'm the worst person in the world."

"Ethan, some people are into birthdays, and some are not. It's no big deal. My dad's not into it. My mom has to twist his arm just to get him on the phone to say 'happy birthday, love you, hon.' Besides, I think I know a way you can make it up to me."

He dropped his hands from his face, intrigued by her suddenly warm tone. "Yeah?"

She nodded and reached for his hand, holding it in both hers as she caressed it. "You could fly fifteen hours, jump out of a plane in the dead of night, rescue me from four armed guards, and lead me to safety."

"Does this time count?" he asked.

"What am I, a used piece of meat? Of course this time doesn't count. I'm going to need you to do it again."

"You are so high maintenance," he said. He brought her hand to his mouth and began kissing her fingertips, but the monkeys overhead grew restless at the movement. Sitting back, he let go her hand and resumed their game.

"What was your first job?" he prompted.

"Math tutor."

"I would have been frigging Michelangelo if you had been my tutor," he said.

"He wasn't a mathematician," she told him.

"And if you had been my tutor, I would know," he said.

"First kiss," she said.

"Yes, please," he said, leaning in.

She put up a hand to halt him. "Who was your first kiss?"

"I want to say it was a girl with a name of some sort, possibly she also had hair and a face."

"You don't remember?"

"There were a lot of girls and a lot of kisses. I was ten and the first of my friends to kiss a girl, that much I remember. What about you?"

"I was twelve, and I was feeling left out because I was one of the last of my friends to kiss a boy. But I was kind of iffy on whether I was interested in boys yet or not, so I grabbed a random boy from my class and kissed him. But I wasn't satisfied with the result. So I kissed him again and then a few more times until I felt I got it right."

"Well, this marks the first time I've ever envied a twelve year old boy."

"He was a little dazzled, poor kid. He followed me around for two years after that, until his family moved away."

"Is Bonvoy your first serious relationship?" he asked.

"I dated a boy for two years in high school. I really thought I was going to marry him."

"What happened?" he asked.

"We were going to go to separate colleges and didn't want the burden of a long distance relationship. It was very amicable, very friendly. We had a nice, rational conversation, wished each other well, and hugged goodbye. Then I went home, crawled into bed beside my big brother, Johnny, and cried for four solid hours while he consoled me."

"Aw, you're giving me the sads. Anyone else?"

She shook her head. "A few months here and there in college, but no one special. What about you? Have you ever dated anyone seriously?"

"If you consider a second date serious, then still no," he said.

She blinked at him. "You've never even had a second date with a woman?"

He blew out a breath. "What do you want me to say here, Amelia? That I'm a player? Fair enough."

"How about that you're scared? That you believe if you let a woman get too close to you, she'll see the real you, beneath the dashing, charming veneer. That maybe she won't like what she sees and she'll go away. So you reject her before she rejects you."

"I thought all that was covered by the player description," he said.

"Am I the first woman who has tried to get her claws into you?" she asked.

"No, but you're the only one who's come close," he said.

She looked away, off into the distance, watching a couple of monkeys in a treetop groom each other. "Don't stop playing. Ask me something else, anything," he prompted.

"When was the first time you lost someone close to you?"

"Before I joined up, no one. After, I don't have enough fingers and toes to count them. What about you?"

"Maggie was engaged to this guy, Sam. He was like a part of our family, a really great guy. We all adored him. He got into a car accident and died two months before their wedding. It was horrible, heartbreaking, and awful." She glanced at him sideways. "Why do you look like that?"

"Because I was blessed with good DNA?" he tried.

"No, you have the same expression you used to get when you tried to pretend you went to Canada on business."

"It's nothing."

She sat up on her knees, looking behind him.

"What are you doing?" he asked.

"Checking to see if your pants are actually on fire."

"Amelia, come on."

"You said you were going to tell me things," she reminded him. She pinned him with a stare, and he actually squirmed.

"It goes against protocol. It goes against everything," he said.

She continued to stare at him until he broke.

"He didn't die," he blurted. "Sam, the guy, he faked his death because he was in a terror cell. When he reappeared, they used Maggie to get to him. Things got dicey, we had to rescue her."

"I remember that. Her cheek was bruised when I came to visit. She wouldn't tell me why. Sam is really alive?"

He nodded. "I saw him myself."

She blinked a couple more times and then burst into tears. "Oh, no," he muttered, reaching for her and trying to soothe her, or at the very least trying to keep her quiet.

"You're upsetting the monkeys," he whispered, and that made her laugh enough to stop the tears.

"I'm sorry. It was such a hard time for our family, for Maggie, and it was all pretend. What she must have gone through, seeing him again."

"It turned out all right. She has Ridge now."

Amelia nodded, sniffling. "If she chose him over Sam, she must love him more than I even realized. I want a love like that." She looked away, blushing. "I mean, you know, someday, with someone."

"I do, too," Ethan agreed. "Someday, with someone."

Just not with me, Amelia thought. She sat back, putting distance between them.

"You're doing the thing again, the pouty girl thing where you withdraw and ignore me," he complained.

"No, I'm doing the human thing where I have an emotion and allow instead of suppress it," she argued.

"That's still a girl thing."

"Why are you not afraid of anything in the world except commitment?" she asked.

"Whoa, going straight for the kill shot there, aren't you?" he said, shifting uncomfortably.

"You jump out of airplanes, you swim unbelievable lengths, you physically rescue people from danger, you shoot guns, you fight with your hands, you have no fear, but you won't return a woman's phone call. Why?"

"Because the other things are, at least somewhat, within my control. If I fail, I'm the only one who gets hurt. If I fail at a relationship, I'm failing someone else. I'm letting someone down."

"That's the whole point of love, to take a risk on someone else. Without the risk, there can be no reward," she said.

"Get back to the game. Ask me something else."

"I'm tired." She pressed her thumb to her forehead. "You ask a question."

"How many men have you said I love you to?" he asked.

"Now who's going in for the kill shot?"

He nudged her. "Still waiting on an answer."

She locked eyes with him. "One. How about you?"

"None. Yet," he said, then he cradled her face in his hands and kissed her.

CHAPTER 17

The kiss had the potential to be explosive, but the monkeys began to chatter. Ethan and Amelia pulled apart to look up, and the monkeys quieted down. They reached for each other again, and the monkeys started to scream.

"These must be Africa's famous chastity monkeys," Ethan noted, and Amelia laughed.

"It's probably for the best. It doesn't seem like the most productive way to spend our afternoon."

"If you think kissing is supposed to be productive, you've missed the point entirely. Kissing is about kissing."

"Kissing is never about kissing," she argued. "Kissing is a question. Is it going to lead somewhere? Is it going to end there? Am I connecting with this person? Is he connecting with me? Could I kiss this person every day for the rest of my life?"

"You have all that running through your head when you kiss someone?" he asked.

"Don't you?" she asked

He snickered. "No. If I hear anything at all from my brain, it sounds like giddy laughter, or possibly someone chanting, 'more, more, more, see how far you can take this.'"

"You're trying to tell me you can kiss any random person without having feelings for her?" She curled her lip.

"Uh, yeah, duh," he said.

"Gross."

"Can I remind you that within the first fifteen minutes we met, you shoved me in a pantry and nearly kissed me unconscious?" he said.

"That was a blip. I told you I didn't normally do things like that."

"When you say not normally, how often have you done that?"

"Including with you?"

He nodded.

"Once. Stop grinning like that."

"Or what? You'll kiss me and make the monkeys scream?" he guessed.

"It might surprise you to know I have never lacked for male attention. I have never once had to pursue a man, they pursue me," she huffed.

"If you think it's supposed to make me feel less cocky that the woman every guy wants wants me, you clearly don't understand men at all," he said.

"You make me so mad sometimes," she said.

"That's passion, baby," he said. He inched up her robe to rest his hand on her leg when a monkey took aim and threw a nut at his head. "Ouch. How do you have all the animals in Africa trained to protect your virtue, Snow White?"

"They're not doing it on my orders. My mom must have gotten to them," Amelia said. She rested her head on his shoulder and closed her eyes. They lapsed into silence a while. The quieter it became, the deeper his thoughts grew.

"Amelia," he whispered after a while. He wouldn't disturb her if she was asleep, but she answered promptly.

"Are you whispering because you're afraid of the monkeys?"

"No. Maybe a little. I have to ask you something."

"What?"

"Do you actually understand what it would be like to be with someone like me?"

"Yes."

"You can't say yes automatically. You have to think about it."

She paused. "Yes."

He sighed. "I'm serious here. I'm gone twenty days of the month, and most of that time is spent in places where there's a good chance I won't come home again. Statistically, I'm already an anomaly because I'm still alive at the ripe age of twenty-eight. When I am home, I spend most of that time dealing with the emotional repercussions of my job. The rates of burnout, depression, suicide, substance abuse, and divorce are off the charts. We've already established I have no framework on how to be in a stable family. I have no idea how to be a husband or father. All I know is the job. I'm a terrible bet."

"Ethan, I know exactly how many days of the month your work takes you away, and though I haven't known exactly where you've gone, I knew it wasn't sunny California for beach time. I realize how hard your job is and the effect it can have on you; I'm getting a taste of it right now. I don't know how you do it, but I'm glad you do because the world needs men like you. But here's something I know that you don't, a secret I'm going to tell you: You live life to the fullest; you give a thousand percent to everything you do. And I know when you finally decide to commit and love a woman, you'll love her with that same all-encompassing passion and devotion. And if it were me you chose to love, I would understand that whatever time we had together was special and unique, that we had lived and loved more in a short amount of time than most people do in a lifetime. Because the things you think make you a bad bet are the things that make you the best bet. Not the safest, but life's too short for safety."

"That was kind of the perfect answer," he said. "Can you do one more thing for me?"

"What's that?"

"Say it in French," he pled.

She complied. He slid his arm around her, and she rested her head on his chest. "I could listen to you read a tax form in French and find it sexy," he admitted.

"Come April, I'll be sure to arrive on your doorstep with a stack of forms from the IRS, just to keep things spicy."

"You probably would," he said. He wouldn't put anything past her. She yawned. "Go to sleep, Melly."

"I don't want to abandon you to keep watch alone," she said, yawning again.

"You're not abandoning me. I'm holding you. There's a difference," he said.

"Maybe just for a minute," she said, curling toward him in a ball so her hands were fisted at his chest.

"Are you comfortable? I can shift, if you like."

"I'm good, except the Kevlar. When I get home, I'm going to invent a bullet-proof vest that's also good for cuddling," she said. "Something warm and fluffy, perhaps in a jewel tone. Black is so last year."

He placed her hand under the vest, on top of his shirt. She did him one better by weaseling under the shirt and pressing her palm to his abs. "There we go," she murmured. "Are you sure you're going to be all right? You're not afraid you're going to fall asleep?"

"I'm good," he said, his tone brusque.

"Are you feeling okay? You sound a little hoarse, and your cheeks are kind of flushed." Her thumb made a little circle around his navel.

"Go to sleep, Amelia," he choked.

"I'm feeling a bit perkier." Leaning closer, she pressed her lips to his neck. Overhead, a monkey took aim and bounced another nut off his skull.

"What are you hitting me for? She's the one making the moves," he hissed toward the trees.

Amelia laughed, withdrew her hand, kissed his cheek, curled back into a ball and rested her head on his leg. With a wary glance at the treetops, Ethan rested his hand on her shoulder.

"They seem okay with that," she whispered.

"That's because they can't read minds," he said.

She smiled, and a few minutes later she was asleep.

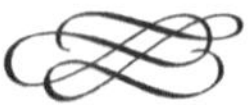

CHAPTER 18

They left just after dark. Ethan became antsier and antsier until finally he said they could leave.

"Are you going to tell me now why you were so jumpy back there?" she asked once they were a safe mile or so away from the border.

"Because night is the safest time for us to get away from people, but the most dangerous time to avoid animals."

"I didn't even think about that. It's like Africa is actively trying to kill us in every possible way," she said.

"There's a lot of good here, a lot of beauty and nice people. We're just not on the sort of journey that sees any of that right now. And my mind is always geared toward spotting the threat." He shifted his weight, flexing his shoulders.

"I can carry your pack for a while, if you want," she said.

"It's heavy," he said.

"I'm strong. I do Pilates," she informed him. "And sometimes hot yoga."

"If I let you carry it, will you show me what hot yoga is sometime?" he asked.

She nodded. They stopped and he placed the pack on her back. "You good?" he asked.

"Gup," she said, stumbling a little. When he said heavy, she had no idea he meant *heavy*. The thing was probably sixty pounds, and he had been carrying it for days.

"Amelia."

"Bimp."

"Why don't I take the pack back and you can regain the ability to form actual words again?" he said. She stood still while he lifted the pack off her back and put it back on his.

Flexing her shoulders, she resumed walking. "Now when people ask me how I got injured in Cameroon, I'm going to have to tell them it was from walking three steps with a heavy backpack. What a wimp I am."

"I spent years training to be able to do the things I do, to condition my body and mind to respond the way I need it to, when I need it to. It's not like I could walk into your salon and give someone a perm on the first try," he said.

"How do you know about perms?" she asked.

"My granny used to get them," he said.

"She might be the only one who still does," she said.

"How did your parents take the idea of their math genius daughter becoming a beautician?" he asked.

"First of all I'm not a beautician, I'm a stylist. Second, they eventually came around. It helped that I had Maggie on my side. My brother, Darren, still thinks I've wasted my life."

"What does he do?"

"He's getting his doctorate."

"In what?"

"How to try to run other people's lives and give unsolicited advice. He's really good at it. It's nice he's found his passion," she said, and he laughed.

"I take it you guys don't get along," he said.

"Do you remember those old *Tom and Jerry* cartoons where they fought incessantly the entire episode? I wish we got along that well. Do you have siblings?"

"I have a half sister, five years younger, your age. We get along okay; we talk a couple of times a year. She'd like to be closer, but you can imagine how that goes."

"You said she's a half. How does that work?"

"My parents got divorced, my dad got remarried and had her. For a while I shunted between the two houses, but then he left that family, too. Thankfully he stopped reproducing, hopefully because he realized parenting wasn't his thing. Not that he was abusive or anything. He was just not father material."

"Are you close to your mom?"

"I talk to her less than I talk to my sister, and she seems perfectly fine with that arrangement. My parents weren't horrible to me. They were just cold, withdrawn, indifferent, into their own lives."

"How did you turn out so well?" she marveled. He laughed before realizing she was serious.

"It's nice you think that, but I'm an unproven quantity, remember? I've never been a husband or a father. I've never even been a boyfriend."

"But you've been a soldier, a hero, a rescuer, a team member, an employee, a best friend. All of those things count for something," she said.

"Where can I purchase your worldview? It seems way better than mine." He took her hand. They walked a while longer in companionable silence, and then it started to rain. Amelia had been in too many rainstorms to count, but this was unlike anything she had ever experienced. Water seemed to come at her from every direction. She could swear it was actually raining backwards, as if coming up from the ground.

"It's the wet season, did I mention?" Ethan yelled. He was standing right beside her, but she could still barely hear him. After only a moment, she was soaked through to the skin, despite the fact that she was wearing two layers. The town was still a couple of miles off. They tried to hurry, but what had been a road a few minutes ago was now ankle-deep mud. The bottom foot of the long robe became quickly caked with layers of wet earth. Eventually, when it became too heavy to walk, Amelia peeled it off and wrapped it around her shoulders.

She thought it would be easier to walk if she took off her shoes, but Ethan stopped her.

"You can't walk barefoot here. Too much bacteria your system isn't used to," he yelled.

She kept her shoes on and inched forward. If not for Ethan taking her hand and practically dragging her along, she likely would have gotten stuck and cemented in place, possibly forever.

The rain showed no signs of ending; it went on and on and on. At last they eked their way into the city, but it was now so late everything was dark. All doors and windows were closed. Somehow through the sheeting rain, Ethan located a church with an attached parish house. He pounded on the door and eventually it was opened by a little man wearing hastily gathered vestments. It seemed to take him a while to recover from his shock at seeing two Americans on his doorstep at what was possibly the middle of the night. Yelling to be heard over the drenching, howling rain, Amelia tried to explain their situation. After a further moment of confused staring, he came to his senses and invited them inside.

They hovered in the entry, rivers of water pooling at their feet. A few weeks ago when they'd gone swimming, Amelia still hadn't been as wet as she was now. Even her ears felt filled with water.

"We were wondering if you have a room to rent for the night," Amelia said at Ethan's prompting. "We'll pay cash, American. And if you have any food, that would be appreciated as well."

The man looked between them. "Are you married?" *Es-tu marié?*

"No," Amelia replied. *Non.*

His face fell. "I am sorry. There is a room, but I cannot let it go to an unmarried couple. A room in God's house is not designed for sin."

Outside the rain was still pouring in waves. She wondered what God had to say about sending two wet, hungry strangers back out into the pouring rain with no prospects, but she didn't argue.

"What did he say?" Ethan asked. Amelia explained to him, and he glanced sharply at the man. She was afraid he would argue or, worse, physically force the man to keep them, but he did something even more surprising. "Ask him if he'll marry us."

"Ask who if he'll what now?" she said, her head swiveling to look at him so quickly she wrenched a neck muscle.

"Just ask," he said.

"Have you lost your ever-loving mind?" she said.

"Have you taken a look outside? Pretty sure I saw some animals lining up in pairs and looking for a boat out there. We need a place to stay. He has a place to stay. I don't see the problem," Ethan said.

"The problem is we'd have to get married."

"I thought that was what you wanted," he said.

"When did I ever say that?"

"You said you love me," he reminded her.

"When does I love you mean let's get married before our first date? There's a timeline for these things and, I know dating isn't your forte, but marriage usually comes at the end, not at the beginning."

"It's not a legal marriage," he explained. "Just a religious one."

"Oh, well, if it's just a religious one…Did the rain wash away your sanity?" she said.

He eased closer, placed his arms on her biceps, and gave them a light squeeze. "Amelia, just ask the man."

Slowly, she turned her head to regard the priest, if he was a priest. She had no idea. "Can you marry us?" she asked, her voice shaking.

"*Oui*," he replied with a definitive nod.

"See? Problem solved," Ethan said.

"Ethan…"

"Amelia, we are never going to find another place to stay in this downpour. The man has a room for rent, I say we jump through this tiny hoop and take him up on it."

"The tiny hoop is a wedding band," she said.

"You're getting caught up in the details. Big picture: we'll have a safe, warm bed for the night. Remember the jungle where we spent ten hours today? Remember how it felt to walk through that mud? Remember how hungry, wet, and exhausted you are? Do you want to do all that again?"

She shook her head.

"Good." He took her hand and faced the man. "We're ready."

The man reached for his bible and performed the ceremony then and there, as they continued to drip water in the entryway. Amelia felt like she was having an out of body experience. Not only was she getting married, but she had to translate the ceremony for Ethan, including his vows. She felt a little like she was marrying herself. At the end, he gave her a chaste, perfunctory kiss while his drenched hair dripped water all over her nose. The priest shook Ethan's hand and showed them down the hall to their room.

"Hmm, not a bad setup for such a small town," Ethan mused as he turned in a slow circle in the middle of the room. Their host left and returned a few minutes later with crackers, cheese, two bottles of Coke, and two clean robes, soap, and a towel.

"You will have to share the towel," he said.

"No problem, thank you," Amelia said on autopilot. She sounded like a robot. Or a nervous bride on her wedding night.

"You can shower first. There's probably only enough hot water for the first one, so go ahead," Ethan offered.

She nodded, dazed, grabbed her stuff, and headed into the bathroom. She tried to shower quickly to conserve warm water for Ethan, but it was already fading by the time she rinsed her hair. She put on the clean robe and returned to the room where Ethan remained standing where she'd left him.

"I didn't want to drip near the bed," he explained and Amelia's eyes turned involuntarily there, toward the bed she'd be sharing with him. Her husband.

After he left the room, she doubled over and rested her head on her knees, trying and failing to draw a deep breath. What was happening here? Was Ethan expecting something to happen? He had said the marriage was in name only, an admitted sham. Did that mean he had no expectations of her?

She stood up. Forget his expectations. What were hers? It was her wedding night, too. For all she knew, she might never get another. The only thing she had to feel guilty about was that she had a boyfriend waiting back home. But she would break up with him, if she could. It wasn't her fault she had no way to communicate with him until they reached the embassy tomorrow. *Tomorrow.* This could be her last night with Ethan.

That was her last thought as he wandered back into the room, sparkling clean and grinning the boyish smile, the one that had first bowled her over on the day they met. "How was your shower?" she asked.

"Brisk," he said.

"I'm sorry. I tried hard to save water for you," she said.

"It's okay. A cold shower was what I needed," he said.

"Why's that?" she asked.

"Because you're obviously not okay with this situation, and I'm not going to force you to do anything you're not comfortable with," he said.

She stood and bypassed him on her way to the door. He grasped her wrist. "Amelia, please don't go."

"Go? Who said anything about go? I'm checking to make sure the door has a lock. We're in luck; it does." She locked the door and turned her back to it, leaning against it.

He looked from the door to the bed and back again. "What exactly happened while I was in the shower?"

"I realized we might never have this night again. So *carpe diem* and all that."

He studied her, his gaze dizzyingly intense. "Are you sure this is what you want?"

She left the door and sauntered toward him, slipping her arms around him when she reached him. "Ethan Becket, Becket Ethan, it's our wedding night. Let's not waste it with words."

"Can I say one more thing?" he asked, his hands smoothing along her waist.

"What's that?"

"*Carpe diem* means seize the day. We want *carpe noctem*, seize the night."

"Knowledge is power. Now let's get cracking," she said. She stood on her toes, her lips met his, and the world fell away for a long, long time.

CHAPTER 19

Amelia usually woke slowly, reluctantly. But the morning after her wedding—and wedding night—her eyes popped open and her brain clicked on as if someone had flicked open her mental shutters. She was nestled into Ethan's embrace, his hand on her hip. How would he view their arrangement, in the light of a new day? For that matter, how did she view it? She had never pictured herself getting married at twenty three. She wanted to establish her career, to establish herself. In the scheme of things, she was still a baby, or so her family delighted in telling her. Her parents still referred to her as "the baby."

To be fair, they weren't legally married. She didn't think a religious ceremony in Cameroon would hold any weight in the states. But wasn't the religious ceremony the most important part? Which mattered more, a commitment before God, or a legalized paper trail?

"Are you awake?" Ethan whispered.

After a fortifying breath, she rolled toward him, uncertain what she would read in his face, but he was smiling.

"So this is marriage," he said. "I don't know why everyone says it's so hard. It's been eight hours, and you haven't gotten on my nerves yet."

"That's probably because we had such a solid foundation to begin with. I bet if everyone got married in a foreign country where one of them didn't understand any part of the ceremony—after zero dating time—there'd be a lot fewer divorces."

"How are you doing?" he asked, his eyes scanning her face.

Terrified and uncertain. "Great. How about you?"

He paused before answering, and she wondered what his brain was saying. "Great."

"What's on today's agenda?" she asked.

"We look for a ride to the embassy. The good news is that we're in the part of Cameroon that's safer and better developed. The drive probably won't be too different from how it is at home. If all goes well, we could fly home tomorrow."

"Tomorrow," she echoed. They had one more day and one more night of feeling as if they were alone in the world together. Tomorrow would be a return to real life, a return to home and family, a return to Piedmont.

"You're wincing," he said, smoothing his finger over her wrinkled nose.

"I really need to break up with my boyfriend," she said. "I'm feeling pretty despicable about that."

"I can't believe you're cheating on such a nice guy," he said. Her lip trembled, and he regretted teasing her. "He'll get over it, Amelia. You guys are dating, not married. We'll buy him a new robe, he'll be fine."

She snuffled a little laugh and mashed her fist to her mouth. "Don't make me laugh about it. I feel terrible; I've never cheated on a guy before."

"This isn't exactly a normal situation," he pointed out.

"Extreme situations are supposed to reveal true character. Mine's not looking too shiny right now," she said.

"Blame it on me, the cad who twisted your arm into marriage," he said. "What's that smile for? By the way, it would be easier if you'd tell me your thoughts instead of making me puzzle through your expressions."

"Of all the people I might have guessed to twist my arm into a marriage, your name wouldn't even have made the list," she said.

"Sometimes in the field, survival requires you to do unbelievable things," he said.

The truth comes out, she thought. It had been a nice delusion that he wanted the marriage for any reason other than as a means of scoring a place to stay, but she should have known better. His goal since the whole ordeal began had been survival. It was ingrained in him to do what needed to be done to make sure the people in his charge made it through alive. Maybe she should be flattered he was looking out for her so intently, willing to go to so many lengths to keep her safe and well. And at least he was being honest. He had never once pretended to be anything other than what had was, had never tried to fool her into thinking he was capable of more. "A true cad would lie about his intentions," she said.

His brow puckered. "Amelia, I have to tell you about my date."

"You don't have to. Your life is your own, Ethan. You don't owe me anything, least of all explanations. I should probably get ready anyway." She tried to ease away from him, but he rolled on top of her, trapping her beneath the full weight of his body.

"Just listen for a minute, please, let me get it out. One time when I was a kid, I tried my cousin's chewing tobacco, thinking it was the awesome new hobby I wanted to pursue. But I accidently swallowed it. It was horrible. I can still remember the taste, and I felt sick for two days. My date was kind of like that. She was pretty and interesting and seemed into all the same things I was, but I hated every minute of it because she wasn't you. In that moment, I wanted you so badly I ached. You made me *ache,* Amelia. And that has never once happened to me before. Ever."

"Oh." His face was a half-inch away, his lips nearly brushing hers.

"Am I crushing you?" he asked.

"Yes."

"Sorry," he started to move away, but she drew him back.

"I never said I didn't like it," she said. She slid her arms around his neck. "What do you think is the protocol for the morning after the wedding night?"

"If we were stateside, we'd probably open presents and start our honeymoon," he said.

"We didn't get presents."

"Lousy, good for nothing friends and family," he grumbled. "Being completely ignorant of our nuptials is no excuse for their stinginess."

"And we're kind of already on our honeymoon," she said.

"I am definitely going to give our travel agent a bad review when this is over," he said.

"So I guess we'll have to forge a new path. Are there any cards in your pack? I'm cutthroat at *Uno*."

"No, sorry. I usually always bring *Uno* with me on assignment. You'd be amazed how it brings terrorists together."

"Not like *Monopoly*."

"Don't mention *Monopoly* here. It's why I can't go back to the Congo," he said.

She rested her foot on his calf, sliding it gently up and down. "I could teach you to crochet. Oh, wait, we don't have a hook."

"We should probably work with what we've got." His fingers stroked down her neck.

"What's in your bag?" she nipped his jaw.

"Spy stuff. We could disassemble my weapon, clean it, and put it back together." He closed his eyes and appeared to be concentrating hard on the conversation.

"I already did that. I woke in the night and couldn't sleep, worrying about it. I can't abide a dirty gun." She kissed his ear.

"I know I'm supposed to say something quippy here, but I can't. My brain can't with the thinking anymore. Please put me out of my misery," he pled.

"How can I do that when I don't know what you want?" she teased.

"You, I want you," he croaked.

She wanted to tell him he had her for as long as he continued to want her, but the words felt too heavy. Instead she kissed him and tried hard to convey everything she was feeling. A long time later, when she had to shake him hard to wake him up again, she thought maybe she'd succeeded.

"I was promised a smooth ride," Amelia said. Once again they had scored another vehicle that seemed to be lacking shocks. Though, to be fair, it may have had shocks at one time that all broke after so many hard trips over rutted roadways. Last night's rain had left even deeper ruts and, in some places, washed away portions of the road entirely. Their driver seemed unfazed by all of it, maintaining the same high rate of speed regardless of the road's condition.

"This is only the first part of the trip. He's taking us to a bigger city where we'll have access to a better car and a better road," Ethan yelled. The wind carried his voice away, but Amelia got the gist.

"Don't know why you want to trade out cars, mate. This one could get you through a war and back," the driver yelled. He was Australian and, unlike the French-speaking natives they'd encountered, seemed to want to have input on everything. Every time Amelia or Ethan spoke, he gave his unwarranted opinion. His name was Jones. Amelia had no idea if it was a first or last name because he had introduced himself as "Just Jones." "Like Cher?" she'd asked, and he had given her a blank look with the reply, "No, it's Jones."

"Jones thinks we should keep this car," Amelia relayed.

"Jones thinks a lot of things," Ethan replied. Jones had spent a long time detailing for them why he thought it was a bad idea for them to honeymoon in Cameroon, as had been their official story. He had also spent a long time expounding on how he would solve the most recent Ebola outbreak in the Congo. Amelia had missed most of that discussion because at the first mention of the disease, she'd pressed her palms over her ears, tuning in at the end to hear him say, "And that's what I'd do with all the leftover blood."

"You're so adorably squeamish," Ethan said.

"No, I merely maintain the crazy belief that what's inside of you should stay there," Amelia said.

"You'd never survive here then," Jones added. "One time I saw this bloke's leg get..."

Amelia had no idea how the story ended because she pressed her palms back over her ears until he stopped speaking. "I could have used the monkeys help much more with him than with you," she noted.

"Monkeys? Ah, no, they're pesky little beasties," Jones announced. "And the diseases they carry. I once saw a bloke..."

Ethan reached over and pressed his palms to Amelia's ears for the duration of the story. "*Thank you,*" she mouthed.

The drive to their first stop seemed unusually long, mostly because Amelia spent much of it with her hands pressed to her ears. "There should probably be a store in this town, if you need anything," Ethan said, removing her palm from her ear as they approached the town.

"Really?" Amelia asked excitedly. She needed everything.

"Ah, no, mate, those stores are for the tourists," Jones interjected.

"Jones, we are tourists," Ethan reminded him.

"Yeah, but I'll show you where the good stuff is, all the animal skulls and monkey paws, yeah? We have to go into the bush a bit, but as long as you've got your gun, you'll probably come out all right," Jones said, giving them an eager glance in the rearview mirror.

"Thank you, Jones, but I'd rather have a comb and toothbrush and not have to use the gun to get them," Amelia said. "Unless of course there's only one left and I have to fight someone for them."

"Ah, you Americans are never up for any adventure," Jones groused.

"We do all right," Ethan said, squeezing Amelia's knee.

"Where'd you lovebirds meet?" Jones asked.

"My sister's house," Amelia supplied.

"I used to have a sister, but then one day she..."

Amelia never learned what happened to the sister because she slipped her fingers in her ears, surreptitiously this time. She didn't want to be rude to Jones, but she was glad she hadn't listened when Ethan turned to her, shell shocked, and whispered, "Remind me to call my sister when this is over."

When they reached the town, Ethan walked Amelia to the tiny little store and deposited her in front of the section that was clearly supposed to appeal to western tourists. There was an oversized plastic comb that looked as if it had been made during the Carter administration along with some lip balm, something with a German title she guessed to be deodorant, a small display of pink lip gloss, perfume from France, and, miraculously, one container of Maybelline mascara. She picked up the tube of mascara and cradled it in her palm. Perhaps it was shallow, but she missed her makeup. She knew she was blessed to have a good complexion and pleasant features, and she didn't take that for granted. But she still enjoyed employing the full power of makeup. The application process always made her feel like an artist at work on a canvas, except the canvas was her face. And she had a modest YouTube following for her tutorials. Nothing that would make her rich or famous, but enough to keep her interested in the hobby.

Despite using expensive, boutique makeup at home, Amelia had always stuck with the same ubiquitous drug store Maybelline mascara. Seeing it now halfway across the world was a pleasant reminder of home. She bought one of nearly everything, minus the perfume that smelled like a lilac bush died and gave its essence to fill the bottle. As she was at the counter to pay, she felt a tiny tap on her leg.

When she looked down, a little boy of about four stood staring up at her. "Can I touch your hair?" he asked in French.

"Of course you can," Amelia said. She knelt on the floor and untied her hair from the hasty braid she'd made to keep it from blowing haphazardly around the car.

"I've never seen yellow hair before," the boy said, smoothing his hand gently over her corn silk tresses. After a few minutes, he lost interest in her hair and his eyes rested on the candy display behind her.

"Would you like a sweet?" she asked. When he nodded, she handed it to him, making eye contact with the storeowner so she would add it to her tab. The boy took the candy but didn't eat it right away. Instead he cradled it lovingly to his chest like an injured baby bird. He might have been older than four, she realized. His head was overly large, as if he had suffered malnourishment in his short lifetime. She made further conversation with him, asking about his home and family.

Ethan returned to the store a few minutes later and saw Amelia still on the floor, the boy beside her. She had her arm around him and they were laughing over something she'd said. He stopped short, almost stumbling back a step, staggered by her beauty and the unexpected impact it had on him. It wasn't that she was pretty, although she was. She had a fresh sort of natural loveliness, a girl-next-door aura. What captivated him at the moment was the glimpse of her inner beauty, on full display as she spoke with the boy. She shimmered with it, radiating kindness and love from every pore.

She caught him looking at her and tilted her head in question, the smile still on her lips.

"Ready?" he said, then cleared his throat and repeated himself when it came out as a halfhearted croak.

She nodded and, standing, gave the boy a little hug goodbye. "Thanks for the store suggestion," she said to Ethan. "I found what I was looking for."

He nodded then rounded the corner with her, herding her into the alley, where he pressed her against the wall and kissed her with all the pent up, confused emotion he'd just been feeling.

"Ready?" he said when the kiss was finished. His forehead was touching hers, his eyes closed.

"For what, exactly?" she asked.

"Phase two," he said, opening his eyes. "I secured us a better car. I think you're going to like this one. Come on." He took her hand and led her to their new car. It wasn't quite a limo, but almost. The windows were tinted black and there was a long, spacious back seat. The wheels had been modified to handle the rough roads, looking more like they belonged on a tractor than a car.

"Sweet," Amelia exclaimed. "This is awesome, it's like going to prom except everyone outside the car seemingly wants to kidnap or kill me."

"That didn't happen at your prom? You must have gone to a posh school," he said, opening the door for her.

"Who's our driver?" she asked.

"About that," Ethan began, but from the front seat Jones turned around and spoke to her.

"All right there, Melly? Find your knick-knacks and girly dos?"

"It's Jones," Amelia said.

"It turns out cars are easier to find than drivers," Ethan explained.

"It's only a frog hop. Just five hours, and we'll be there," Jones said.

"Five hours," Amelia repeated. "I can't hold my hands over my ears for five hours, Ethan."

"Come on, Melly, this is the good part of the trip. Right roads, and all," Jones said.

Ethan tapped him. "You don't call her Melly; that's what I call her."

"Right, that's what you call her. And that's what I call her," Jones said.

"But I call her that. I'm the only one who calls her that," Ethan protested.

"You patent the name, gent?" Jones asked.

"I think you lost this one as soon as we opened the door and got inside the first time and he asked if he could sniff us," Amelia said.

"But..." Ethan started, but she interrupted him.

"Ethan, the man keeps a stuffed kangaroo in his pocket, and I'm not sure he doesn't know it's not real. So I think it's okay to let this one go."

"As I told you before, we don't have ready access to medical care here. It would be dead helpful to have someone who could sniff out infection and make a diagnosis, yeah?" Jones said, shamelessly eavesdropping on them again. "And I know the kangaroo's not real. It's in memory of a real kanga I used to know. He met a bloody end one day when..."

Amelia started to put her hands over her ears, but Ethan intercepted her. "Let me show you the car's best feature." He pressed a button and a glass divider went up between them and Jones. Better still, it was also tinted.

"Can he see us back here?" Amelia asked.

"No, I checked," Ethan said.

All the windows were tinted; no one could see them.

Amelia eased closer and slipped her arms around him. "You know what I want to do right now?"

"I think I do," he said. "You want to take a nap."

She nodded, yawning.

He eased her into his lap and kissed the top of her head.

"I'm sorry. It's just so cozy and warm, and I'm so sleepy," she said, yawning again.

"It's almost like you didn't sleep well last night," he said.

"Strangely, I feel like I hardly slept at all, like I ran a marathon for a few hours. Can't imagine why," she said.

"Jet lag finally catching up with you, probably," he suggested.

"If that's jet lag, I'll become a record holding frequent flier," she said, and he laughed.

The divider rolled down. "All right back there, mates? Sounded like a sea bird choking on a biscuit."

"Ethan was laughing," Amelia explained.

"I'd have that looked at if I were you. I knew a bloke who sounded like that, and it turned out his lung was..."

Ethan pressed Amelia's head to his chest, covering her exposed ear with his hand. "Go to sleep, I'll take one for the team and keep listening," he whispered.

"You are literally the best," she said. She closed her eyes and, a few minutes later, she was asleep.

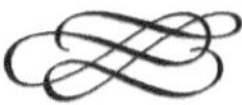

CHAPTER 21

"Are we staying at the embassy?" Amelia asked. They were approaching Yaounde, the capital of Cameroon and also the location of the nearest US Embassy.

"No."

"Why are we going there?"

"We have to get your replacement passport," he said.

"Um, I don't have a passport," she said.

"Of course you do, but it was stolen, along with our luggage, and so now we have to get you a new one," he said.

"How am I getting a phantom passport?"

"A certain azure-haired friend is arranging some things, creating some records, etcetera."

"Blue can do things like that? I thought he was just comic relief," Amelia said.

"No one actually knows the extent of what Blue can do, or exactly where he came from. Like all good hackers, he just appeared one day. Rumors say he was created in a chat room," Ethan said.

"Maybe he's part of the matrix," Amelia suggested.

"Maybe we're the matrix, and he's the only thing that's real," Ethan said.

"I've seen him sing karaoke. Believe me when I tell you he's unreal," Amelia said.

"Look, the city's coming into view," Ethan said, pointing.

Amelia gasped. "It's huge, and it's so modern." So far the parts of Africa she'd seen were what she'd imagined—rural and underdeveloped. But Yaounde looked like any city in the US. "Is that a Hilton?"

"There are a lot of hotels here. They get a lot of dignitaries from all over the world. There's a big expat population here, too. Both US and French," he said.

"Wow," she said, her face pressed to the window.

"Africa is diverse and fascinating. You haven't gotten a good taste of it," he said.

"Next time I get kidnapped, I'll ask to be taken to one of the nicer parts," she said.

The car came to a halt so suddenly Amelia slammed into the seat in front of her.

"Jones, what gives?" Ethan asked, rolling down the divider.

"This is as far as I go, mates," Jones replied.

"The embassy's over a mile away," Ethan said.

"This is as close to it as I get. There's a lot of law around there, if you know what I'm saying," Jones said.

"I think we do," Ethan said. He paid the man and gathered their paltry luggage—his pack and her small paper bag from the store.

"I don't understand his meaning," Amelia said.

"He's wanted," Ethan said.

"For murder," Jones added. "But it wasn't my fault, yeah? This bloke took a spear and got it lodged in his..."

Amelia was already out of the car and down the street by the time he got to "bloke."

"We spent eight hours being driven by a murderer," she said when Ethan caught up to her.

"Africa's kind of like the old west in the US. It's a good place to get lost and be anonymous if you're on the run from the law," Ethan said.

Hand in hand, they walked to the embassy where they were greeted by two marines, one of whom Ethan knew.

"Thompson, I didn't know you were here. When did you leave Nigeria?" Ethan asked.

"Last month," Thompson said. "What are you doing this far south? I thought they kept you in the north." His gaze turned curiously to Amelia.

"This is Amelia," Ethan introduced.

"Amelia," Thompson said, his tone warming with interest as he turned to face her.

"My wife," Ethan added, and Thompson blinked in surprise.

"I didn't think guys like you had those," Thompson said.

"Guys like what?" Amelia asked, feigning innocence as she slid her arm around Ethan's waist.

Thompson froze, realizing he may have bumbled into revealing classified information. "Guys who, you know, travel a lot and..."

"It's all right. I know Ethan works at an indexing firm that has a strong interest in northern Africa's wellbeing," Amelia said.

"Right," Thompson agreed, nodding in relief.

"Keep it together, Thompson. Don't let the sun melt your brain," Ethan advised. "Jarheads," he added to Amelia, rolling his eyes.

"I'd make a comment about you navy girls, but you don't even have that going for you any more," Thompson said, buzzing them through the gate.

"He does all right," Amelia said. Ethan laughed, and the two men fist bumped good-naturedly.

"What's our story?" Ethan prompted Amelia after they headed through the gates.

"We came here to get married and someone stole our luggage and my passport," she dutifully recited.

"And why did we come to Cameroon to get married?" he asked.

"Because you didn't want an ordinary wedding; you wanted an adventure," she added. "You know that makes you sound insane."

"Remember Jones? That's the type they're used to dealing with here. Believe me, they'll think nothing of it," he said.

"If they're the good guys, and you're the good guy who was doing a good thing to rescue me, why can't we tell them the truth?" she asked.

"Because they don't run on good intentions; they run on the law, and I broke a few dozen of them to get here and get you out. Never, ever forget we're not in the United States anymore. I mean, for the minute we are because we're at the embassy. But you see what I'm trying to say. We're in a country with different laws. We have to function within the very strict parameters they've set up."

They were shepherded through multiple channels of security until finally landing in the office that would help them with Amelia's passport. "Amelia Eldridge, ah, yes, I received word from the State Department you would be arriving for a replacement passport." The man, Mr. Bauer, paused and looked at her over the paperwork before him. "Usually I'm the one who has to contact them. I rarely remember them contacting me and sending the information first." He stared at Amelia as if waiting for her to offer an explanation.

"I have family connections," Amelia said, her heart pounding. "My uncle."

"I used to work at the State Department. Who's your uncle?" Mr. Bauer asked.

"He doesn't actually work at the State Department. He's just well connected," Amelia said, squirming. Ethan's hand slid to rest on her knee, giving it a pat. He had told her to say as little as possible, to let him handle it. *I lie for a living. It's harder than it looks.*

"Washington's a small world. Who is it?" Mr. Bauer pressed.

"The Colonel," she blurted.

He smiled patronizingly. "Which one?"

"Colonel John Caruthers," Ethan inserted smoothly. Mr. Bauer flinched and actually seemed to pale at the mention of the name. "Yes, good, well everything seems to be in order here, though no one told me you were here to get married."

"It was spur of the moment," Ethan said. "We came to vacation, and I talked her into it."

Amelia wanted to blurt things. She had never been good at deception, and now words and assertions wanted to blather out of her like hot lava. She sat on her hands, trying not to say anything else. *Keep it simple,* Ethan had warned. *Good liars take a spark of truth and stick to it. Bad liars elaborate. Resist the temptation.*

In her mind, all kinds of concocted stories were swirling, detailed, fantastical excuses for why she and Ethan had come to Cameroon and what they'd done since they'd been there. One of them involved pirates, a search for hidden treasure, and possibly a dolphin rescue. *Don't talk, don't talk, don't talk,* she warned herself.

Her passport was in his hand. All he had to do was stamp it, and they could leave, but he seemed content to linger, to chat. "You're a well-traveled young lady," he said, staring at her passport.

"I am?" Amelia asked and then, when he gave her a questioning look, "I mean, I love to travel so much it doesn't feel like I've been that many places." *Or anywhere ever.*

"I'd say eleven countries by the age of twenty three counts as widely traveled," Mr. Bauer said. "Twelve, including Cameroon." He stamped the passport and handed it over.

Amelia nodded, not trusting herself to speak again. Ethan wrapped things up with the man, recounting all the fun, make-believe adventures they'd had in Cameroon. It sounded like complete gibberish to Amelia, but Mr. Bauer ate it with a spoon.

"And when do you head back?" Mr. Bauer asked.

"Day after tomorrow," Ethan said, surprising her again.

They shook hands with the man, thanked him for his help, and then they were on their way.

"Day after tomorrow?" she questioned when they were safely outside. "I thought you said we were leaving tomorrow."

"When I was describing all the fun, made up things we'd done, I felt a little bad we hadn't actually done those things," Ethan said.

"You want us to go back and re-do the trip so you won't feel guilty for lying to the embassy?"

"No, I felt bad for you, that your entire time here has been fear and worry and hunger, hiding, and escape. So I was thinking tomorrow maybe we could have a day of fun."

"That sounds suspiciously like a honeymoon," she said.

"Not to me. Anytime I pictured a honeymoon, it didn't involve leaving the hotel," he said. "Speaking of which." He put up a hand, hailing a taxi. Once they were tucked inside, he gave the driver their destination: "Hilton, *s'il vous plait.*

Outside it was growing dark. Amelia stared up at Ethan's handsome profile, her heart flip flopping around inside her chest, and added her own direction to the driver. *Va vite:* go quickly.

CHAPTER 22

Amelia sat in the lobby of the Hilton, staring at her passport while Ethan secured their room. Why had Blue made up so many differing country visits for her? It seemed to go against what Ethan told her, to keep it simple. To further the lie, she would have thought Cameroon would have been her first and only stamp.

"Ready?" Ethan asked. She tucked her passport in his pack and followed him to the elevators that took them to their room.

"A king size bed," she exclaimed when he held the door and allowed her to precede him inside. She took off her shoes and flopped on the bed, stretching out her arms and legs as if about to flap them and make a bed angel. Ethan took off his shoes, set down his pack, and lay down beside her.

"It takes so little to please you," he noted.

"I wish I could have a king size bed, but my apartment is microscopic. Before I got my own place, I spent four years sleeping on a dorm-room bunk bed. And the last couple of nights, I shared a bed with you, giganthor. Muscles are all well and good until they take up two thirds of available space. Might want to dial down the 'roids, just saying."

"I have news for you: you were the one chasing me all over the bed.

I've never felt so hunted. Every time I tried to find some space, you were on me like a lamprey checking for parasites. I thought it was some kind of commando cuddling technique, but you were dead asleep. You're sleep needy." He poked her.

"I'm like a heat-seeking missile when I sleep. I go where the action is." She reached out and ran her fingers gently through his hair.

She had a tiny mole on the right side of her forehead. He noticed it for the first time a couple of days ago, along with a small birthmark on her right shoulder. He had never been with a woman long enough to notice details like that before. In the past he'd imagined making those types of intimate discoveries might make him feel panicked or trapped. Instead he was surprised to find it gave him a little thrill, as if he'd stumbled upon a hidden secret only he knew. It satisfied some primal urge within him, of both possession and belonging.

"You're staring at my forehead so hard I feel like you're trying to hypnotize me. If I start clucking like a chicken whenever anyone says the word 'tortilla,' I will not be pleased."

"You have a cute little mole right there." He pressed his finger to her mole.

"Okay," she said, her tone uncomprehending.

"We should probably make some calls," he said.

"About my mole? Because I've had it forever, so please believe me when I tell you no one's interested."

"I need to check in with work, and you need to check in with probably everyone you've ever known who is worried about you," he clarified.

"Oh, right. That." How could she have forgotten her family? They must be panicked by now.

Ethan went first. His conversation was odd and cryptic, a series of statements she guessed to be some kind of code. When he was finished, he dialed for her because she had never made an overseas call before. Her mother picked up on the second ring.

"Hi, honey. How's your trip?"

She frowned at Ethan in confusion, but as he couldn't hear her mother's side of the conversation, he had no idea why. "Good," Amelia drawled.

"We couldn't believe it when Maggie told us you were jaunting off to Africa, spur of the moment. I guess her love of travel is starting to rub off on you."

"Yeah," Amelia said. Maggie hadn't told her parents she'd been kidnapped? She wondered why.

"You sound tired, sweetie. Are you getting enough rest?"

Amelia glanced at Ethan. The last couple of nights had been sleepless, but she wasn't complaining. "There's a big time difference here."

"Which country are you in? If Maggie told me, I don't remember."

"Cameroon," Amelia replied. "They speak French here."

"Oh, that explains a lot. I'll have to tell Darren you're getting some use out of that minor," her mother said, laughing.

"How's Johnny?" Amelia asked.

"He's doing really well. Cam put a bug in his ear about trying the Special Olympics this year, so we're looking into which category best suits him. So far we haven't found one for enthusiastic high fiving," her mother said.

Amelia smiled. "Mom, it's really great to talk to you, but I have to go."

"Sure, honey. Thanks for calling. Maggie warned us we probably wouldn't hear from you until you got back, so this is a nice surprise. Enjoy the rest of your trip."

Amelia's gaze landed on Ethan again. "I definitely will. Love you."

"Love you, too." They disconnected.

"All right?" Ethan asked.

"She didn't know anything was wrong," Amelia said.

"Is anything wrong?" he probed.

"No."

"Well, there you go. Ready to talk to Maggie?"

"Ready," Amelia said. He dialed for her again, and Maggie answered after one ring.

"Amelia?" Maggie said.

"How did you know?" Amelia asked.

"I don't get as many calls from Africa as you might expect," Maggie said, and it sounded as if she was crying.

"I'm fine," Amelia assured her. "Perfect in every way, except some minor sun damage on my face. If I get wrinkles, I'm definitely suing the blood diamond people."

Maggie laughed and sniffled. "It's so, so good to hear your voice. How's Ethan?"

"Equally perfect," Amelia said. She turned her back to him, afraid her tone might reveal something to the sister who knew her too well.

"Uh-oh," Maggie said, reading between the lines anyway.

"No, it's fine. We're friendly."

Behind her, Ethan snickered. She put her hand in his face and pushed. Ignoring her, he brushed aside her hair and began kissing her neck. She closed her eyes, trying hard to maintain the thread of the conversation with her sister. "How's the dog?"

"The best little baby ever." There was a commotion in the background. "Every time I call him our baby, Ridge feels the need to remind me he's not. But he loves his daddy so much. Every new baby brings adjustments."

"Soon your baby is going to be a hundred pounds," Amelia reminded her.

"More of him to love," Maggie said. "Although we may need a tad of obedience school because he destroyed one of Daddy's leather loafers and left a rather unpleasant present in the other. Hey, I almost forgot to ask. When are you coming home? Did you get a flight out tomorrow?"

"We're coming home the day after tomorrow. Ethan has some business to attend to first," Amelia said.

"I'll say I do," Ethan whispered.

"Have you talked to Piedmont?" Maggie asked. "He's been a mess since you went away."

Amelia tensed, and Ethan stopped kissing her. "Not yet."

"Call him soon, the poor guy," Maggie urged.

"Yes, okay. Hey, I have a couple of questions for you. Blue made me a passport and put all these obscure countries on it. Any idea why?"

"Knowing him it's for some reason that makes sense only in his twisted mind," Maggie said.

"Why didn't you tell Mom and Dad the truth?" Amelia asked. "That I'd been kidnapped."

"That was my first go-to panic reaction, but Cam rightly pointed out there was no need to alarm them unnecessarily when the probability Ethan would successfully retrieve you was so high. You're in good hands there."

I'll say I am, Amelia thought. Her eyes landed on Ethan's strong, capable hands, and she picked one up, bringing it to her lips.

"Send us a message when you know your travel arrangements, and we'll meet you at the airport," Maggie said.

"Will do. Before I forget, how was France? What did you guys do there?"

"I couldn't begin to tell you," Maggie said, her words weighted with meaning.

"I want a rundown of the food in person," Amelia said.

"That I can do," Maggie promised. They said their goodbyes. Amelia hung up the phone and sat staring at it a moment.

"Is there anyone else you'd like me to dial?" Ethan asked. His hand was still in hers, his finger sliding gently over her palm.

"Yes, okay, I supposed I'd better," she said dully.

"Can I give you a piece of advice, man to woman?"

"What's that?"

"Resist the temptation to confess or break up over the phone. You're five thousand miles away, and he's been going out of his mind with worry over you. Be soft, be gentle, and tell him face to face when you get home."

"That's good advice," she conceded. "Maybe you should write a book: *How to Break Up With Your Boyfriend, One Man's Guidance for his Wife.*"

"Pretty sure I'm the last person who should be doling advice, dating, marital, or otherwise." He dialed the phone and sat back, blatantly eavesdropping.

"Taking a page from Jones's book, are you?" she asked.

He grinned and spoke in an exaggerated Aussie accent. "One time I knew this bloke who got a phone jammed in his…"

"Hello, Amelia, is that you?" Piedmont asked. She had instructed Ethan to dial his private line, the one he kept on reserve for friends, family, and her.

She turned her back to Ethan. "Hi."

"Oh, my…are you okay? I can't tell you how worried I've been. Hold on, I have to sit down. I think I might pass out. Okay. Are you all right? Please tell me you're all right."

"I'm fine, honestly," she assured him.

"Amelia, I am so, so sorry. If I'd realized how credible the threat was, I would have had the security team start immediately. They assured me there was no way they could get to you."

"Piedmont, stop, please. It's really not your fault."

"Yes, it is," Ethan hissed. She waved him away.

"These have been the worst few days of my life," Piedmont wailed. Amelia closed her eyes. *These have been the best days of my life,* she thought, shocked. How could she think that when it had been nothing but constant danger? She glanced at Ethan. *Oh, that's how.*

"When you get home, promise me we'll have a conversation about us," Piedmont demanded.

"I promise," Amelia said, the weight of guilt hanging like a stone in her gut.

"Take care and, Amelia, I love you."

She hung up without saying another word and sat stock still, the phone cradled in her lap. Ethan eased forward and took it away from her, setting it aside. Then he pulled her close and hugged her, and that was when the dam burst and she cried.

"I'm the worst person in the world," she wept.

"Of course you're not. It's a really big world," Ethan said.

"Do not tease me about this," she pled.

"I'm sorry, but how can I feel bad when his loss is so much my gain?" he asked, his arm smoothing gently up and down her spine.

"What's even the point when you don't want anymore than these few days?" Finally, she broached the question that had been weighing on her.

"You said time wasn't a factor. You said however long we had together would be enough, that it would be special and unique because we would have loved more in the short term than most people do in a lifetime."

"What are you, a human tape recorder?" she asked, pushing at his chest in irritation.

He pulled her back again, holding her close and pinning her arms when she tried to squirm away. "We have tonight, tomorrow, and tomorrow night. Let's enjoy them for what they are. If you will give me that much, I swear to you we'll have fun and you won't regret it. Will you?"

After a moment's hesitation, she nodded. "But I feel gross, enjoying ourselves on Piedmont's dime."

"So do I. That's why I put the hotel on my credit card," he said.

"You did?" she asked.

He nodded. "The rest of the trip is on him. It *is* his fault you're here, his case, his failure to warn you, to properly protect you. But this part, this is for us, this is ours."

"Oh," she doubled over, clutching her chest.

He rested his hand on her back, alarmed. "What is it?"

"I got this huge rush of emotion, so big and so sudden that it physically hurt for a second. Or maybe it was that mystery food we ate from the unlicensed street vendor. But I'm pretty sure it was love."

"Do you want to kiss me or throw up right now?" he asked.

"Kind of both, but I think kissing is winning," she said. She sat up on her knees and advanced on him, knocking him back onto the bed as she tackled him. They kissed for a while, and it was definitely leading somewhere other than food poisoning when Amelia suddenly sat up and reached for her passport.

"I figured it out," she said, waving the passport in Ethan's face.

"What?" he asked. His brain was having trouble catching up to the fact that she was no longer in his embrace and using words.

"Why Blue put all the random countries on my passport. If you take the first letter from each country, it spells out a message." She showed him, and he read out loud.

"You owe me big."

"I can't believe he made up eleven fake country visits to send me a secret message. No wonder he sent me to Oman twice," she said, smiling at the passport in recognition of Blue's skill as a prankster.

"This was what you were thinking about as I was kissing you?" Ethan asked.

"Among other things."

He plucked the passport from her fingers and tossed it onto the nightstand. "Let's try this again and in fifteen minutes, if you're able to think of anything at all besides me and what we're doing here, I've failed in my objective."

Fifteen minutes later, she pulled away to say two breathless words to him: "Mission accomplished."

CHAPTER 23

He bought her a dress. Men had bought her gifts before—flowers, chocolate, and the like. Piedmont had even given her a ridiculously extravagant pair of sapphire earrings she now felt compelled to return. But in Ethan's case it felt like something more, mostly because she guessed he had never bought a woman anything. Not only did he buy it for her, but he got up early while she was still sleeping, checked the size in the tag of her t-shirt, sneaked to a local merchant, and returned in time to surprise her with it when she woke. It was a simple white cotton sundress, but to Amelia it was better than anything she'd ever owned because it was imbued with so much meaning.

Now that she had a modicum of makeup and access to a hair dryer, she spent a while in the bathroom getting ready so that when she emerged clean, fresh, and wearing the new dress, she felt a bit like an actual bride. Ethan must have thought so, too, if his awed reaction was any indication. He was so enthusiastic about her appearance in the new dress that he promptly removed it. Two hours later, they began again and finally left the hotel.

They went to a museum and strolled hand in hand, enjoying the artwork. When that was finished, they strolled through streets and shops, stopping to look, but not to buy. It might have felt like any day in DC except Amelia was the only one who could understand what people were saying. When they grew hungry, they went to an upscale, sit-down restaurant, the first non-street food they'd had in days. When the meal finished, they walked hand in hand back to their hotel, talking and laughing. A boy of about fourteen passed them and then, without warning, grabbed Amelia's wrist and yanked her to him, holding a knife to her side.

"Money." His accent was so thick, it was clear he had learned the word for the sole purpose of robbing English-speaking tourists. Amelia could read the expression in Ethan's face, could foresee the complete destruction he was about to reap on their unsuspecting robber.

"He's a boy," Amelia said. "A child."

Ethan took a breath, and then another. Slowly, his fingers relaxed and unclenched. "Tell him I'm a mercenary who works for *Les Irakiens de Bonaloka*. Tell him you're their property, and if he doesn't get his hands off you, they'll destroy him and his entire family."

Amelia relayed the information. Before visiting Africa, she never imagined listing herself as anyone's property, nor that it would keep her safe from being mugged. But it worked. The boy dropped her and ran off, a terrified expression on his face.

"Do you want to tell me why that worked?" Amelia asked, straightening and brushing her dress.

"The group I listed is a gang in Doula. They're more terrifying than anything I could have done to him. Are you all right?"

"I'm fine," she assured him.

"I've been with other civilians in the field, and you're by far the calmest," he noted.

"They must not have known or trusted you like I do," she said. "I'm safe with you, I know that."

"Thank you for that, and thank you for stopping me from destroying that kid. It would have been a terrible thing to live with."

"You're welcome."

"The only problem is that I have all this unspent adrenaline rushing through me. I'm afraid I'm going to need an outlet."

"I could show you some Pilates," she suggested.

"I think I'd prefer that demo on the hot yoga," he countered.

"I'd need heat and steam for that," she said.

"I have a few suggestions about how to make some," he said, holding the door to their hotel for her.

Later that night they lay in bed, sleepy but not ready for sleep, both cognizant of the fact that this was their last night, that tomorrow they would leave Africa and get back to reality.

"You're a really good first date," Amelia said, her finger trailing gently over Ethan's chest.

"I'll say I am," he agreed, and she laughed.

"Tomorrow..."

"Nope. Not going to think or talk about tomorrow," he said. "We agreed we would enjoy the time we had together. No strings, no talk about the future. Just us, just tonight."

"That sounds like a reject greeting card that got sent to the discount store because no one bought it," she said.

"New dream: retire from the agency and work for Hallmark's rejected card division," he said.

"Maybe if we don't fall asleep, tomorrow will never come," she said.

"Try it," he said.

"I will," she agreed and, twenty minutes later, she was asleep.

♥

*I*n the morning, they were both quiet. Ethan watched Amelia in concern as she seemed more subdued than usual.

"Are you feeling okay?" he asked.

"I have a bit of a stomach ache. It's fine," she assured him, but he wasn't sure. She barely spoke three words to him as they packed up their meager belongings and took a taxi to the airport. The flight would last nearly twenty-four hours, including layovers. When they arrived at the airport, Amelia disappeared into the bathroom and was gone so long they nearly missed their flight.

"Amelia, seriously, are you okay?" he pressed once they were finally seated and settled.

"I'm fine," Amelia assured him, though she looked pale.

When they arrived at their first layover, she disappeared into the bathroom again for a long time. After she emerged, she bought a soda.

"Amelia," Ethan began, but she held up a hand to halt him.

"I'm fine, really, everything is fine. I feel a little yak, but I'm good. Sorry to be a downer on the last leg of our journey," she said. They sat in front of a television, spouting news in another language. "Which country are we in?"

"Brussels," he said. "More use for your minor."

She smiled weakly and rested her head on his shoulder. He took her hand, and she fell back asleep.

On the last leg of their journey, back to DC, he caught her wincing a few times, but every time he called her on it, she insisted everything was fine. Finally he'd had enough and snapped at her.

"Clearly you are not fine. Could you please tell me what's going on?"

"I feel a little crampy, okay? I've sort of lost track of where I'm at in my monthly schedule, and I can't remember if the timing is right. And it's making me feel sick to my stomach. Aren't you glad you asked." She tore open his pack and searched for the antacid she'd purchased at the last airport.

"Yes, cranky pants, I am. If you're not doing all right, I want to know about it."

"Why? Because you're my husband for," she checked his watch, "two more hours?"

"One more hour," he corrected.

"Stupid military time," she groused, unrolling an antacid tab and popping it in her mouth.

"I want to know because I care about you and your wellbeing, regardless of the status of our relationship," he said.

"That's another card for your rejected Hallmark collection," she said, leaning forward and gasping slightly as another pain hit.

"Amelia, you are not okay," he insisted.

She frowned at him, but she was in too much pain to contradict.

When they landed in DC, they were the first ones off the plane. Amelia didn't think much of it until they were met at the end of the tunnel by Maggie, Ridge, and two medics wheeling a gurney.

"You ordered an ambulance?" Amelia said, turning to stare up at Ethan in dismay. "I told you I'm fi….." She doubled over and grasped his arm, biting back a scream as a wave of pain so intense washed over her, she feared she might pass out.

"You seem totally fine, but get checked out for my sake, please," Ethan said sarcastically as he put his arm around her and half carried her to the waiting medics. "She was really good until this pain started a few hours ago," he added, addressing Maggie and Ridge.

"I'm good," Amelia tried to assure them with a thumb's up. Then she groaned and clutched at her stomach, ruining the effect.

"Come on, we'll get you checked out. You'll be right as rain in no time," one of the medics said.

"Is there any chance you might be pregnant?" the other EMT asked as his partner began buckling her onto the gurney.

"Yes, but only by a couple of days," Amelia said and, as one, Maggie and Ridge swiveled to look at Ethan.

"I got nothing," Ethan said, shrugging helplessly.

CHAPTER 24

"Ethan," Maggie exclaimed.

"It's not as bad as it sounds," Ethan said, directing the remark to Ridge.

"If you think I'm the one you should be afraid of, you've clearly never seen Maggie angry," Ridge said.

"How could you…you went to get her and…she's vulnerable, and you took advantage…" Maggie sputtered.

"Sweetheart, you've gone to that place only dogs can hear," Ridge said, stroking his fingers soothingly down her arm. "Let's hear what he has to say."

"Long story short, we got married," Ethan blurted.

They stared at him, unblinking. "I think we're going to need the long story," Ridge said.

So Ethan explained how everything came about. When he was finished, Maggie seemed more subdued.

"Do you like me again?" Ethan asked her, tapping her foot with his.

"I'm processing, and I'm a little sad, honestly. We didn't get to have cake," Maggie said.

"I'll buy you a cake," Ridge offered.

"It's not the same if it's not wedding cake," Maggie said.

"We still have wedding cake in the freezer. We'll have some when we get home."

She bit her lip. "You might want to recheck the data on that."

"Maggie, you ate our wedding cake without me?" he asked.

"I was having a bad night. It was right before I had to re-up my qualifications, and I was nervous."

"And you thought the solution to being nervous about having to re-qualify on your physical was to eat a quarter of a sheet cake the night before?" he said.

"Apparently yes because I passed," she said.

"You passed because I spent the month beforehand training you," he said.

"Maybe it's because you trained me, or maybe it's because I ate the cake. There's really no way to know for sure."

Ridge picked her up under one arm and shook her up and down. "This is what happens when you marry an Eldridge woman, Ethan. You're never sure if you want to spank her or kiss her."

"Um, hello, I'm being wheeled to an ambulance here," Amelia called as the medics led her away.

"I'll go with her. You guys do your post-mission decompression thing," Maggie offered.

Ridge and Ethan looked at each other. "How was the mission?" Ridge asked.

"Good," Ethan said. "What else does she think we do?"

"I'm not sure, but in her mind it probably involves crying and maybe singing and some kind of craft," Ridge said.

"Huh," Ethan said, ending in a face-splitting yawn.

"Are you sure you want to go to the hospital? I could take you home," Ridge said.

"I'll go to the hospital, make sure she's settled," Ethan said. He fell asleep as soon as they were in the car. Now that they were back and Amelia was safe, he could let go and relax. Being constantly vigilant for days on end caused an unfathomable level of exhaustion.

When they arrived at the hospital, the emergency room would only allow one person to be with her. Maggie was already there, so

Ridge and Ethan waited in the lobby. Ethan fell back asleep almost immediately. He felt as if he hadn't slept in years, and it was comforting to have Ridge beside him again, keeping watch.

Finally she was admitted and they could see her. "Did they say what's going on?" Ethan asked when they entered the room.

"Not yet. They've been running tests and doing scans. Hopefully we'll hear soon," Maggie said.

"How are you feeling?" Ethan asked Amelia, going forward to perch on the edge of her bed.

"Ethan!" she exclaimed, her voice light and loopy.

"Did they give you something for the pain?" he guessed, smiling.

"No, it just went away. It's magic," Amelia said.

"They put something in her IV," Maggie said.

"Magic," Amelia insisted.

"You're high as a kite right now, huh?" Ethan said.

Amelia shook her head. "I don't do drugs."

"I think someone did them for you," he said.

"Don't tell my mom," she pled, pressing her finger to her lips. "Shh."

"Our secret," he agreed, mimicking her gesture and pressing his finger to his lips.

"And don't tell her what we did in Africa," Amelia continued. "And don't tell Maggie."

"I don't think I have to," he said.

"You're so handsome, and I love you so much," she blathered, smooshing her hand along his cheek. "Why can't I feel my fingers?"

"Because you're high," he reminded her.

"I don't do drugs, crack is whack," she said, then, "Shh, don't tell my mom."

"I won't," he promised, smoothing the hair away from her face. He needed to go home, to shower, to check in with work, to sleep, but the thought of leaving her, even under Maggie's watch, was painful. She had been in his care and his alone for so many days. Giving her up felt like the end of something.

"Ethan."

"Hmm."

"I might throw up."

"It's okay," he said.

"You won't like me if I throw up," she said, starting to cry.

"I will, I promise," he said.

"No," she shook her head. "Pretty girls don't puke."

"You might want to tell that to some sorority girls I met once," he said. "Why don't you try to get some sleep?"

She clutched at his shirt. "I think they put something in my IV, something bad."

"It was to take the pain away," he explained.

"It didn't work because it still hurts right here." She pressed her finger into the bed.

"I'm sorry your bed hurts. How about I'll give you a kiss goodnight, and then you'll go to sleep," he suggested.

"You are so good at kissing, and all the other stuff we..." he pressed his lips to hers, cutting her off. When he pulled away, she dutifully closed her eyes and fell asleep.

The doctor entered immediately after. He spoke at full volume. Amelia stirred and woke but didn't speak. "You are her sister," he said addressing Maggie.

"Yes, and that's her husband," Maggie said, tossing Ethan an impish smile because she knew it would make him squirm to hear the new title out loud, and it did.

"Ah," the doctor said, turning toward him. "That explains things."

"Explains what?" Ethan asked, his heart thundering. How could he have possibly messed things up already?

"Amelia had an ovarian cyst that ruptured," the doctor said.

"Is that serious?" Ethan asked.

"No, but it's painful," the doctor said.

"Was it from being on the airplane, the altitude?" Ridge asked.

"No, ah," he glanced at Ethan again. "Sometimes vigorous, er, activity can precipitate a rupture."

"Oh, geez," Ethan said. Ridge snickered and ducked into the hallway.

"Really glad my mom was not here to hear that tidbit," Maggie said.

"I didn't note any other cysts in her scan, so things should be fine going forth. No need to scale back, er…"

"Good, thanks, we get it," Ethan said, holding up his hand to halt the man speaking. It was a mercy he had a high threshold for embarrassment.

"We'll keep her overnight, monitor her pain, and she should follow up with her gynecologist after release. Otherwise I think she'll be fine," the doctor said.

They thanked him and he left the room.

"So, I should get going," Ethan said, his eyes on the blank television.

"Here's Amelia's key. Why don't you swing by her place and pick up a few things before you come back tomorrow. You are coming back tomorrow, yes?"

"Yes," Ethan said. He held out his hand and she dropped the key into his palm. He chanced a glance at her, but she looked away.

"No eye contact for six weeks. It's the TMI rule," she said.

"Right, good," he agreed, standing.

"Ethan," she said, and he paused. "You know this makes you my little brother now. You should be prepared because I'm going to bring the hammer, and you will feel the pain."

"You're only ten months older," he noted.

"And I won't let you forget it until I'm forty, and then we'll never speak of age again," she said.

"Good enough," he agreed, mussing her hair while still carefully avoiding her eyes.

CHAPTER 25

It seemed Ethan had barely left the room when Piedmont entered, a large bouquet under one arm. Maggie had texted him before the bombshell marriage announcement, but he had been stuck in court and unable to get away. Now of course she regretted the contact, but she couldn't leave him hanging when he had been so worried for so long.

"Hey, how is she?" he asked, his eyes and tone filled with worry.

"She's fine. It was a cyst on her ovary that ruptured. It caused a lot of pain, but she'll recover completely," Maggie told him.

"A cyst ruptured? What causes that?" he asked, and Maggie choked, turning away to cough into her hand. The noise woke Amelia who stared up at Piedmont, blinking in confusion.

"Hey, bunny," he said, moving closer to the bed to smooth the hair away from her face.

"Piedmont-t-t-t-t," Amelia said, seeming to get stuck on the last syllable.

"How are you feeling?" he asked.

"T-t-t-t," she continued to stutter.

"They gave her something for the pain, perhaps a bit too much," Maggie said, squinting at the IV to try and read the label. Whatever it was, she planned to request it next time she had to be in the hospital. Perhaps even if she was just going as a visitor. Whatever it was, Amelia was flying high and feeling no pain.

"I'm going to stay here with her tonight, make sure she's okay," Maggie said.

"I think I should stay," Piedmont said.

"Um, yeah, that's really nice, but you've had court all day. I'm sure you're exhausted," Maggie said.

"I've been going out of my mind for days, and now that I have the chance to be with her again, I'm not going to waste it," he said.

"I think she would feel more comfortable having me here, in case she gets sick or something. She hates throwing up in front of people," Maggie told him.

"I'm not exactly people, and I'm going to see her throw up eventually."

Maggie began to sweat. There was a good reason he was a topnotch litigator. But this was an argument she couldn't lose. Her sister was *married*. There was no way she could let her boyfriend stay the night while Amelia was unaware. Who knew what she might say or do? In her current state, she could marry Piedmont. Plus she knew Amelia wouldn't want him there when she came back to her right mind.

"I'd feel more comfortable if I were the one here," Maggie said.

"I don't want to pull rank on you, but I'd rather be the one to stay," Piedmont said.

"In the scheme of rank, I think sister is higher than boyfriend," she said. In the past, she might have given in and backed down because she hated confrontation and disagreement. But Cam had taught her a thing or two about standing strong and not backing down, and she wasn't going to lose.

"I may be her boyfriend now, but we both know it's headed someplace deeper," Piedmont said.

"Until that time occurs, I want to be the one to stay," Maggie said.

"Why don't we ask Amelia what she wants?" Piedmont suggested. They turned to look at her while she eyed them owlishly, blinking slowly, one eye occasionally going crossed before straying back into its lane.

"A half hour ago she asked me to buy her a wallaby, so I'm not sure she's the best judge of what she wants right now," Maggie said.

Piedmont leaned over the bed and took Amelia's hand. "Amelia, who would you rather have stay with you tonight, me or your sister?"

"Ethan. I want Ethan," Amelia replied. She tried to sit up and look around. "Where did he go? Why did he go away?"

Piedmont stood looking at her a few seconds and then released her hand. "Well, that was unexpected."

"She's had a rather intense week, and they've been together nonstop," Maggie hedged.

"I get it, Maggie, I've met the guy. I could see how a woman like Amelia could be bowled over by that sort of protective masculinity, and I'm sure it didn't help matters that he was literally her rescuer. I guess my question is do you think it's permanent?"

"I think this is something you need to talk about with Amelia," Maggie tried.

"Do you think it's permanent?" Piedmont demanded in his best *Law and Order* tone.

Maggie nodded. "I think it's permanent."

"No one gets perms anymore," Amelia muttered.

Maggie gave her a pillow. "Take your wallaby." She took the pillow and cuddled it close. "I'm sorry, Piedmont. I'm sure Amelia will want to have a conversation with you, one on one, when she's lucid again."

"What's the point of that?" he asked. "I worry he'll break her heart. He doesn't seem like the kind of guy who will stick around."

Maggie didn't say what she knew about Ethan—that he was slow to make a decision but, once committed, would never go away again. The question in her mind was whether he had actually made that sort of commitment to Amelia or if it had all been part of the heat of the moment of the mission.

"I think this is the first time I've ever not gotten something I wanted," Piedmont said, his tone dismal.

"I'm sorry," Maggie said, although she couldn't actually relate to a nearly thirty-something man who was only now facing his first disappointment.

"I'm not really sure what to do now," he said.

"You go on, minute by minute, day by day, and then suddenly you look back and it doesn't hurt so much anymore and you realize you've moved on," Maggie said.

He blew out a breath and, reluctantly, turned and walked away. Maggie waited until he was gone and then flopped onto the bed beside Amelia, stretching out, drained of all energy.

"That was definitely above and beyond the call of duty. I don't think it's anywhere in the sister code you're supposed to break up with her boyfriend for her," Maggie said. "Ugh, I feel terrible, and I'm not even the one who broke his heart."

"Jones knew a bloke who got a stick lodged in his heart," Amelia muttered.

"What?" Maggie asked. She turned to look at Amelia and was answered by a few soft and gentle snores.

CHAPTER 26

The next morning Amelia awoke alone in her hospital room, confused but feeling better. She reached for the remote for the television, but Maggie arrived before she could turn it on, a bakery box tucked under one arm.

"Hey, you're awake. I had some croissants delivered for us."

"Oh, my lands, you're precious," Amelia said, reaching eagerly for a chocolate croissant.

"How are you feeling?" Maggie asked.

"Good but foggy. Everything yesterday seems like it was being pulled through a layer of tulle. Did they give me something for the pain?"

"Enough to take down a pregnant rhino, apparently," Maggie said.

"Oh, no, did I embarrass myself?"

"No, you were cute. The embarrassment came from other quarters," Maggie said. "Do you remember the doctor being in here?"

"Vaguely. He said I had an ovarian cyst, right?"

Maggie nodded. "He also told us his theory on why it ruptured."

"Why it ruptured..." she mused, thinking. "He said vigorous activity and something about Ethan...oh, oh no. I'm so sorry you had to hear that."

"Sisters don't have secrets," Maggie told her.

Amelia quirked an eyebrow at her. "Really?" Maggie was holding on to a treasure trove of secrets.

"Okay, not secrets like that," Maggie amended.

"Was Ridge in here, too?" Amelia asked.

Maggie nodded, and Amelia groaned. "Don't worry about it. After so many years in the navy, there's nothing he hasn't seen or heard. Besides, with the way those two are with the competition thing, my biggest concern is that Ridge is going to try to one up Ethan by rupturing a cyst on both of my ovaries."

Amelia laughed and clutched at her stomach. "Oh, don't, it still hurts when I laugh."

"Sorry," Maggie said. They finished their croissants in companionable silence before she spoke again.

"Was Piedmont also here, or was that a dream, as I'm desperately hoping it was?"

"Piedmont was here. Good news, you guys broke up, and I'm fairly certain I let him down easy," Maggie said.

"Thanks. And sorry."

"Don't mention it." She paused. "So, you're married."

"I wasn't aware you knew that part, too," Amelia said. "I guess we really do have no secrets."

"Weren't you going to tell me?" Maggie asked, trying not to sound wounded.

"I would if I thought it was going to stick," Amelia said, using the back of her hand to swipe at her eyes.

"What makes you think it won't?" Maggie asked.

"Come on, Maggie. You know him."

"Yeah, I do, and I've never seen him the way he is with you. And Ridge has known him forever, and he said the same thing. Besides, who could let go of a catch like you?" Maggie reached for a tissue and handed it to her. "Come on, Amelia. Pull yourself together. Know your worth. If Ethan knows a good thing when he sees it, he'll get himself together. And if he doesn't, there's nothing you can or should do to change his mind."

"You're right," Amelia said, wiping her eyes. "It's been a long, exhausting week."

"I know, but you're home and safe and loved and everything is going to be okay, I promise you," Maggie said.

Amelia nodded and reached for the bakery box again. "How come you only got four?"

"I thought maybe you wouldn't be hungry after being sick," Maggie said.

"Why? My stomach didn't rupture."

"I'll bring you something else on the way home from work, if you're still here. If you get out early and you need a ride, call me and I'll come get you."

"I'll be fine. Stop mother henning me," Amelia said, hugging her tightly.

"I think we can both agree you've given me good reason this week to be a tad overprotective," Maggie said.

"Maybe a bit, but I'm fine now, I promise. I'm done rupturing, both physically and emotionally," Amelia said. "How was France?"

"Beautiful but totally confusing. I could definitely have used your language skills," Maggie said.

"They kind of came in handy for me this week, too," Amelia said.

"Oh, right the CAR and Cameroon used to be under French rule," Maggie said.

"Your inner nerd is showing," Amelia said.

"You're the one with the inner nerd. Mine is on full display at all times," Maggie said.

"Sometimes I forget," Amelia said. "But that reminds me. You're due for a refresh."

"Of what?" Maggie asked.

"Everything."

"Why can't I find one look and stick with it forever?" Maggie asked.

"You know how Aunt Pat has a Dorothy Hamill and all her clothes have shoulder pads?"

"Yes."

"That's why," Amelia said.

"Fine, but you're going to have to fix it with Ridge. After he saw the bills from the last refresh, he turned on ESPN and went catatonic for four hours."

"So?"

"So that's his equivalent of eating his feelings. He didn't want to be angry I spent so much, but he couldn't get on board with it, either. Combining finances is tricky business. I thought I was frugal and conservative, but the man has a twenty-year plan for our spending and all these flowcharts for kids' college and retirement and paying off our mortgage."

"Sounds intense."

"It is, but it's also nice, to be taken care of, to know he's thinking and planning for our future."

"You guys make it look so easy," Amelia said.

"I'm glad you think so. We love each other, and we're best friends, but we still have to work hard on our relationship. Love's a verb, not an automatic guarantee. We have to choose each other every day in a thousand different ways, and I'm way, way more selfish than I realized."

"You're not selfish at all," Amelia protested.

"That's because you're not married to me. Believe me, it's ugly. But he loves me anyway, and that's the miracle of marriage."

"I want to be like you when I grow up," Amelia said.

"What a coincidence; I wish I had been like you when I was a kid," Maggie said. "Call if you need anything. I can be here really quickly."

"I will," Amelia promised. They hugged once more, and Maggie left. Amelia turned on the television and drifted back to sleep. When she woke again, Ethan was leaning in the doorway, a giant sack slung over his shoulder.

"Are you starting the deliveries early this year, Santa?" she asked.

"What's up, Snoop Dog? Are you still Willie Nelsoning it?" he asked.

"It's possible they made my dose a tad too high yesterday," she said. "What's in the bag?"

"Maggie suggested I pick up a few things from your apartment."

"I think that bag contains more things than I actually own," she said.

"I've seen your shoe collection, so I know you're lying," he said. He entered the room and sat on her bed, setting the bag on the table beside him.

"Don't ask me to give up my shoes for you, Ethan. I've known them longer," she said.

"What would you give up for me, if I asked?" he mused.

"Anything, if I believed your reason was sincere," she said.

He reached into the bag and handed her a toothbrush. She squealed. "You are the best, thank you."

"If a toothbrush makes you that happy, you're too easy," he said.

"I'm pretty sure the doctor confirmed that for everyone last night," she said.

He groaned. "I was hoping you were too doped up to remember that part."

"I really wish Maggie and Ridge hadn't been here to hear it. Now he and I can't make eye contact for six weeks."

"The TMI rule," he added.

"Exactly. Hey, good news, though. They came in early this morning to tell me everything else was clear. No apparent jungle diseases." She paused. "Also, I'm not pregnant. I asked them to do a blood test to make sure."

"Was that a particular concern for you?" he asked.

"Yes. I mean, it's not exactly in my nine-month plan. I finally just got enough in my savings account to cover an extra month of rent. I'm not yet what you'd call financially stable. I'm still getting established in my career, I live in a one room studio...the reasons not to become a mother right now are endless."

"You know I'd support you. I wouldn't leave you or our child out in the cold," he said.

Our child. Despite not being ready, she shivered at the effect the words had on her. "I also didn't want to be pregnant for your sake."

"My sake? Why?"

"Why? Because I don't want you to feel trapped. Or, worse, feel like I'm the one who trapped you," she said.

"That's what you think, that I'd feel trapped?"

She nodded.

"You know what my reaction was when the EMT mentioned pregnancy as a possibility? Unmitigated glee. I suddenly had the chance at something I didn't know I desperately wanted. If anything, I feel bad because I'm the one who trapped you."

"What are you talking about? You didn't trap me."

"I pushed you into a marriage you weren't ready for," he said.

"You were trying to take care of me, to ensure we had a place to stay," she said.

He put his hand over his eyes. "Please don't say that. It makes me feel even worse."

"Why?" She tugged his hand away from his eyes.

"I would never marry someone for the sake of a mission, never marry a woman for a place to stay. We could have stayed in any house in that town if we flashed enough money. Was it nice and convenient to get out of the rain? Yes. Did I feel safer staying at a parish house? Yes. Was it necessary to marry you that night for any reason?" He shook his head.

"Then...why?"

"Because I'm an all-or-nothing person. I either stay on the ground or jump out of the plane. The thought of getting into a relationship, of dating, of arguing, of slowly trying to combine my life with someone else's, of giving someone control, of sharing my space, the thought of everything that could go wrong, it scared me. Bad. I didn't want to fail at that, and especially not with you. But all of a sudden that night I saw a solution, a way out. We could skip all the dating and jump right to the marriage. It seemed like such a good plan at the time."

"But now you don't think so," she surmised.

He shook his head.

"Oh. I guess there's nothing we need to do, since we aren't technically married," she said. She blinked quickly, trying to push back the tears. There would be time to cry later. For now, she would be calm, stoic, reasonable, mature.

"Or maybe we could come up with a new plan," he suggested.

"I'm listening."

"I brought you something else." He reached into the bag and handed her a toaster. "You're right, it's basically all I have, and it's not much, but if you want it, it's yours."

"That's the plan? To give me your toaster?" she asked.

"The toaster and a few less tangible things. I was thinking maybe I could suck it up, act like a man, and date the woman I'm in love with, the woman of my dreams, my wife. And maybe after a proper time of getting to know each other, of courting you and taking you on dates, of calling you for no reason other than I miss the sound of your voice, of kissing you because you're pretty and I want to, of trying to figure out why my apartment smells like dirty gym socks and how your apartment is the size of a closet yet miraculously holds ten thousand pairs of shoes, maybe get re-married in front of our friends and family, legally and officially."

"I'm starting to like maybe," she said.

"Yeah?"

She nodded. "And you've nearly convinced me."

"Nearly's sounding better to me, too. What can I do to take it over the top?" he asked.

"Ethan, since the moment I met you, we've had this explosive chemistry, a crazy attraction that scared us both with its intensity. To counteract it, our relationship turned into a giant game of trying to outdo each other, of one upmanship. And so I guess what I need from you is to hear those three little words, the three words I know you've never said to anyone else."

"That's it? You want to hear me say the words?"

"I *need* to hear you say the words."

"If I say them now, are you going to need me to keep saying them?" he asked.

"No, say them once, and that will be enough," she prompted.

He took a fortifying breath and closed his eyes. "You beat me."

"That was even better than I dreamed it would be," Amelia said. "Now kiss your secret wife, sailor."

He reached for her, but didn't kiss her right away. Instead he spent a while looking at her, studying her face, smiling. "This is going to be fun," he declared.

"Always," Amelia agreed. He kissed her then, but a minute later she pulled away. "But it's kind of a big deal, our marriage in Cameroon. How are you with keeping secrets?"

"I do all right," he said. "Is that what you were thinking while I was kissing you?"

She nodded. "Were you hearing giddy laughter?"

"The giddiest," he said.

"It's really hard to turn off my brain," she told him.

"Let me help you try," he said and, setting aside the toaster this time, he reached for her again.

A while later she pulled away from him again to say two words in a breathless whisper: "Mission accomplished."

Thank you for reading *The Angel and the Agent,* the second book in the Spies Like Us series. For more books, please check out my website www.vanessagraybartal.com

ABOUT THE AUTHOR

Vanessa Gray Bartal is a foodie who spends her time trolling bakeries and dreaming of new ways to use sourdough. When she is not baking (or eating), she loves to make music and spend time with her husband, three children, and sheepadoodle in rural Ohio. Her dream is to fill her books with enough coziness and warmth to brighten someone's day and make them smile. She would love to hear from you on Facebook or through email.